The Death
of the
Brown
Americano

The Death

of the

Brown
Americano

José N. Uranga

iUniverse, Inc.

New York Bloomington

The Death of the Brown Americano

Copyright © 2010 by José N. Uranga

This is a work of fiction. All of the characters, names, incidents, organizations, and dialogue in this novel are either the products of the author's imagination or are used fictitiously.

iUniverse books may be ordered through booksellers or by contacting:

iUniverse
1663 Liberty Drive
Bloomington, IN 47403
www.iuniverse.com
1-800-Authors (1-800-288-4677)

Because of the dynamic nature of the Internet, any Web addresses or links contained in this book may have changed since publication and may no longer be valid. The views expressed in this work are solely those of the author and do not necessarily reflect the views of the publisher, and the publisher hereby disclaims any responsibility for them.

Front book cover photograph image is used by kind permission of the New Mexico State University Library, Archives and Special Collections.

ISBN: 978-1-4502-6698-7(pbk)
ISBN: 978-1-4502-6699-4(ebk)

Printed in the United States of America

iUniverse rev. date: 11/16/10

For Joan

Contents

Buenavida Family Tree

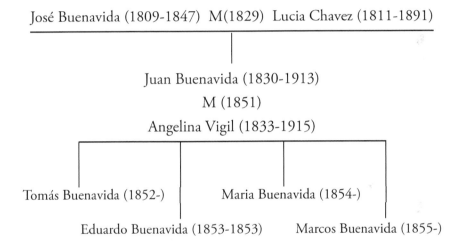

José Buenavida (1809-1847) M(1829) Lucia Chavez (1811-1891)

Juan Buenavida (1830-1913)

M (1851)

Angelina Vigil (1833-1915)

Tomás Buenavida (1852-)   Maria Buenavida (1854-)

Eduardo Buenavida (1853-1853)   Marcos Buenavida (1855-)

Map of Spanish Land in North America (pre-1848)

Map Handdrawn By Juan Buenavida
based On His Recollection of the Arredondo 1670 Map
at the National University, Mexico City

Map of the United States
Following Mexican-American War (Post 1848)

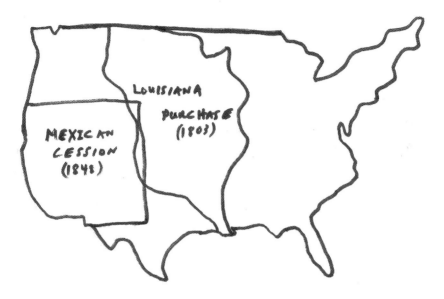

Map Handdrawn By Juan Buenavida
based on Eastern Newspaper Maps

Map of Territory of New Mexico

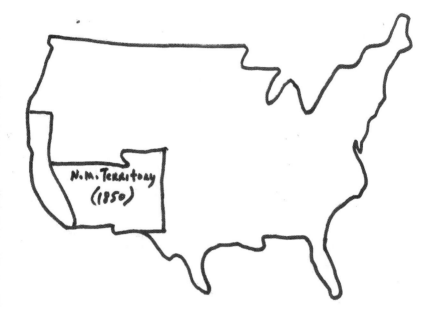

Map Handrawn By Juan Buenavida
based on Eastern Newspaper Maps

"WHAT'S PAST IS PROLOGUE" —Shakespeare

FORWARD

The Death of the Brown Americano, although a work of fiction, is, on the whole, based on historical fact. It focuses on the fictional Buenavida family from its arrival in the southeastern part of the New Mexico territory in 1850 through the early 1900's. The book explores the family's struggle to survive despite the challenges of discrimination, an indifferent government, and harsh economic times. The book explores how the Buenavidas strive to hold on to their Hispanic culture and language while adapting to being "Americanos" in their new country. This work follows on the The Buenavida Dilemma (2003).

BELIEVE EVERYTHING HAPPENS FOR A REASON.

—Unknown

CHAPTER 1
THE FALL

JUAN BUENAVIDA SENSED he was floating, but with no frame of reference. Everything around him was totally black. It reminded him of the several limestone caverns he had explored in the nearby Guadalupe Mountains as a young man. He had once intentionally extinguished his torch on those subterranean adventures and remembered that it was so dark he could not see his hands in front of his face.

While he seemed to be floating, he also felt as if he was ascending in the dark and quiet. It was so quiet Juan could hear his heart beating- deep inside. Suddenly, Juan experienced (sensed?) a flash of light from somewhere above him- a brief illumination yet as bright as nearby lightning in a black, starless and moonless New Mexico night. Then, it was jet black again- but in that brief flash Juan had seen himself as a young boy. A young boy walking hand in hand with his father at the old Rancho Buenavida in what was then Mexico. Then, Juan was floating in the blackness as before, but his right hand felt as if his father had just squeezed it.

Juan sensed he was again moving up in this unlimited blackness-what was happening to him he wondered? Before he could conjure up a thought, another bright flash of light suddenly surrounded him. This time Juan glimpsed himself as a young man at the National University in Mexico City- as a student in a classroom. He had been 17 or 18 then, he thought, as he was enveloped in the obsidian again. Yet, the musty smell of the adobe buildings of the university seemed to linger in his nostrils.

Before Juan could begin to consider what he had just seen, another flash of light shot up around him. While Juan felt blinded by the light and the simultaneous return to blackness, his mind's eye quickly saw Juan on his wedding day- he was holding Angelina's hands as he looked into her eyes. In the darkness now, Juan could still see Angelina's hazel-green eyes smiling back at him with their glints of honey flashing.

NOBODY SAID LIFE WOULD BE EASY; THEY JUST PROMISED IT WOULD BE WORTH IT. —Unknown

CHAPTER 2
THE COMA

ANGELINA VIGIL de BUENAVIDA was frightened. A doctor had been summoned from the village of Loving and was expected shortly. Her Juan was in their bed after having been found unconscious on the ground near their rancho's western perimeter, his horse nearby.

Angelina feared for her husband. While he was 83 years old, he had been in good health. Even though Juan's full head of hair was now salt and pepper and his face was tanned and lined, Angelina still saw the young, handsome man with the twinkling light brown eyes she fell in love with. Yet, he had not spoken or moved since he had been found, placed on a wagon and brought to the house. Angelina had cleaned the deep gash on Juan's head and using her "curandera" (healer) skills, she had applied an herbal salve before bandaging it.

In the September mid-afternoon light, Angelina noticed the dust motes as they danced in the bedroom window light's air. She was holding Juan's left hand as she waited for the doctor. Also in the room were their children: Tomás, Maria, and Marcos. Juan's brothers and sisters had been notified and were on their way.

As Angelina held her husband's hand, she occasionally would squeeze it, hoping for a return squeeze. Nothing happened. Juan's hand was calloused and rough- a reflection of the hard work required to operate their rancho. Yet Angelina knew these hands could be tender and caressing as when Juan had held their infant children or her.

Angelina silently prayed to the Virgen de Guadalupe asking her intercession to revive Juan, to have him recover fully. Angelina forced herself to focus on Juan's recovery- she didn't want to dwell on the alternative of his death. A life without her husband was beyond her comprehension.

Angelina thought of the two family cemeteries- the Vigil's and the Buenavida's. Both were on prominent hills on the two respective ranchos. Visiting her parents' gravesites on their respective birthdays, Angelina could easily see the extent of the Vigil rancho which her brother now owned. She recalled her family's decision to start the family graveyard on that specific hill— her father had loved to ride there and look over his rancho from that perspective. One of her earliest memories of her father was of his silhouette on that hill at sunset- the bright, golden light seemed to turn him into a golden statue. She later learned that this same phenomenon was the cause for the conquistadors' several fruitless searches for "Cibola", the rumored "Seven Cities of Gold", in northern New Mexico which turned out to be sunset- gilded Indian pueblos made of adobe.

SOMETIMES IN THE WINDS OF CHANGE,

WE FIND OUR TRUE DIRECTION. —Unknown

CHAPTER 3
THE RIO PECOS ALIANZA

SHORTLY AFTER THEIR arrival, Juan had realized how vulnerable they were. A small group of Hispanic farmers and ranchers surrounded by large Anglo ranches to the north and west, renegade Anglo raiders from Texas to the east, and the constant fear of Comanche and Apache Indian raids.

With the help of the Vigils, Juan and Angelina convened a meeting of all their Hispanic neighbors shortly after the Buenavida home was completed. All fifteen Hispanic families had attended.

After introductions had been made, Juan decided he should state his concerns directly—there existed a complacency that needed to be shocked into reality. "Compadres", he started, " we are in a very dangerous situation. We have no protection against Indian raids since the two closest U.S. Army forts, Fort Stockton to the south and Fort Sumner to the north do not even patrol our area. The second most immediate threat is the state of Texas which now claims this part of the territory of New Mexico. Remember that the Republic of Texas invaded New Mexico in 1841 claiming it owned all of New Mexico's land east of the Rio Grande ".

"But our governor Manuel Armijo and his militia kicked out los Tejanos in 1841", interjected Luis Carrasco, a horse rancher.

"You are correct Luis", Juan replied. "But Texas still claims all lands in the New Mexico territory east of the Pecos River and many of us live in this disputed area. Our other concern, Juan had continued, should be the renegade Texan bandidos who have raided our area stealing our livestock and killing our people who resist. We cannot count on the U.S. Army to protect us. Remember that New Mexico was invaded by Stephen Kearny in 1846 and annexed to the U.S. before the end of the Mexican-American war in 1848. Also remember that in 1847, 200 U.S. Army soldiers from Fort Union in Las Vegas marched to Taos and crushed the Hispanos and Pueblo Indians who had rebelled against the harsh Anglo rule there. In fact, the Anglo government was so hated that the first Anglo governor, a Charles Bent was killed at his Taos home as part of the rebellion. All houses in Taos were burned and many Hispanos and Pueblo Indians were killed by the U.S. Army".

"So what can our little group of fifteen families do"? asked Tomás Hernandez, a cotton farmer.

Juan had paused before responding until everyone was focused on him and anticipating his response. "I propose we form an Alianza comprised of all our families", Juan had stated as he looked directly at Tomás. "This Alianza would have two main purposes: self-defense and mutual assistance. We need to develop an alarm system so we can all quickly come to the aid of any of us who are attacked. Our farms and ranchos are not that far apart that a signal, such as two gunshots, could not be heard".

Alfonso Sanchez, a quiet sheep rancher, stood and addressed the group. "While I agree that we do need an Alianza such as Juan proposes, I worry that los Americanos will get angry with us forming it. Do we want to trigger their anger"?

Alfonso's question caused several in the meeting to shake their heads or look down at their boots in discomfort.

Fighting to keep his voice calm, Juan had responded. "Compadres, we have to stop thinking of ourselves as second- class citizens and only the Anglos as being Americanos. We are all Americanos or U.S. citizens as a result of the 1848 Treaty of Guadalupe Hidalgo. We are no longer Mexicanos or Españoles. We must start calling ourselves Americanos. If it is easier for you, start calling me "the brown Americano". Many people had laughed. Juan had continued. "I know some of you hold Spanish or Mexican land grants as the basis of title to your lands. The U.S. government promised in that treaty to recognize those land grants. Others, such as the Buenavidas, plan to seek 160 acre federal donations of land or homesteads which we can then legally own after working that land for four years. The U.S. Congress has offered such free land to all citizens of the New Mexico territory that were here before 1853. New Mexico, as you all know, became a U.S. territory in 1850 when Congress refused to admit it as a state.

"Now despite what I have just said about the treaty, the U.S. Congress has decided that land grant holders must prove up those grants with a survey and written records. We must help each other to file those proofs with the Surveyor General in Santa Fe and get them approved. If not filed and approved, you will not own your lands as far as the U.S. is concerned. You land grant holders may want to also seek homestead lands as a backup. An Alianza can help us all succeed by pooling our money and hiring an attorney if needed. Already, we hear that the Surveyor General is denying land grant applications and as a result Hispanos are losing their lands to Anglos".

Luis Carrasco spoke up again asking, "Juan, how else can such an Alianza help us"?

"In several ways", Juan had replied. "We could coordinate our firewood and "viga" (pine tree beams) collection trips to the Guadalupe Mountains. We could help each other with barn- raising or water well drilling. I am willing to translate all papers written in English for any member who can not read English. We can also agree on the values for our barter system of exchange for our goods".

After two hours of discussion, Juan had asked for a vote of all households on whether to form an Alianza. An unanimous vote resulted in the Rio Pecos Alianza being formed. An alarm signal of three consecutive gunshots was agreed upon.

ALWAYS KISS ME GOODNIGHT. —Unknown

CHAPTER 4
THE WEDDING

MANY OF THE relatives and friends had left the Buenavida home after the doctor from Loving had diagnosed Juan's condition as a coma possibly caused by a concussion from falling off his horse. When Angelina and the family had pressed him, the doctor reluctantly admitted that he did not know how long Juan would remain comatose or if and when he would recover. The doctor was certain, based on his examination, that Juan was breathing well, was not experiencing pain, and did not seem to be aware of his surroundings. The doctor also told the family that he doubted Juan could hear or feel anything. To avoid his choking, the doctor strongly advised the family not to feed Juan. The doctor requested he be summoned if Juan's condition changed.

As Angelina continued her vigil by her husband's side, she reflected on their life together. Their courtship had been short—long walks with Juan while being accompanied by a maternal aunt or her mother. An occasional "baile" (dance) allowed close dancing and whispered endearments beyond the hearing of the chaperone. Angelina looked forward to the dances as she thrilled to the new sensation of feeling

Juan's body next to hers. Juan was almost six feet tall and this caused Angelina's head to rest on his chest. Despite the music, Angelina thought she could hear Juan's heartbeat as they slowly danced. "He takes my breath away", she shyly confided to her girlfriends.

The wedding had been small and its date set by the circuit priest's schedule. Juan's brother Marcos was best man and Angelina's best friend, Consuelo, was the maid of honor. The newlyweds moved into the Buenavida home and displaced Lucia, the matriarch, from her bedroom. She had insisted saying she would share a large bedroom with Juan's sisters.

Angelina blushed as she recalled her wedding night. Her mother had not prepared her virgin daughter, but farm girls are not ignorant of procreation. Juan had been a gentle and informative lover. Angelina had been amazed by her new sensuality and how Juan had brought her to orgasm that first night.

Angelina had Mercedes, Juan's lover at the university, to thank for her sexual happiness. Juan had later confided to Angelina that this Mercedes, a widow at thirty, had seduced him through the convenience of their both being boarders in a large home near the university. It had been Mercedes who had instructed Juan, a teen-aged country boy and a virgin, in the ways of pleasing a woman and how a woman pleases a man. Angelina's button at the top of her Venus mound, Juan called it his "friend", had been Juan's pathway to her sexual fulfillment. Angelina had often silently thanked Mercedes, wherever she was now, for her timely seduction and instruction of her husband.

Angelina also recalled how she had insisted on one condition to her acceptance of Juan's marriage proposal. She had told Juan that all married couples have arguments in their lives but she wanted her parents' custom agreed to by him. She smiled in recalling Juan's surprise at her raising a condition to his proposal and that the condition somehow related to her parents. She had quickly allayed his concern by telling him that her parents had the custom and practice of always kissing each other goodnight despite whatever had transpired or been said that day. Juan had then quickly kissed her and told her that he would be pleased to perpetuate that custom with her.

Angelina glanced around her bedroom and saw her children and some of her grandchildren sitting along the walls. Yes, she and Juan had been blessed by God with good children. Juan had been very patient with them and her in teaching them English. His insistence on purchasing newspapers even when money was tight and having the entire family read them had expanded not only their language skills but also their appreciation of events far beyond their small rancho in southeastern New Mexico.

IF YOU SEE WHAT IS RIGHT

AND FAIL TO DO IT, IT IS EITHER FROM A LACK OF

COURAGE OR PRINCIPLE. —Confucious

CHAPTER 5
PROTECTING LAND TITLE

LUIS CARRASCO WAS one of Juan's closest friends and a neighbor ranchero. It was the third day of the vigil following Juan's accident.

"Comadre Angelina", Luis requested permission to speak, as he sat in one corner of the Buenavida bedroom. Angelina was now accustomed to the testimonials friends and relatives were increasingly invoking. Angelina, dressed all in black, nodded to Luis.

"Señora Buenavida, family and friends, my friend Juan lies here in a coma as we all pray for his recovery. I hope he can hear us as we gather around him because we all owe Juan a large debt of gratitude. In fact, without his leadership, we would not own the ranchos of our families. Yes, let no one forget that it was Juan who learned of the 1854 federal law granting patents to 160 acres of land to all of us who were here before 1853- all we had to do was live on and work the land for four years".

"It was our friend Juan who had us then pool our monies so we could all apply for our patents together and prove to the Surveyor General in Santa Fe that we met the law's requirements. Plus several of our families had Spanish or Mexican land grants as their ownership base. Juan's advice was to include those land grants in our Santa Fe strategy which proved to be successful. Yes, that was the beginning of our Rio Pecos Alianza".

"While New Mexico finally became a state last year, we should not forget the blatant actions of the U.S. Congress to delay its admission. We all know the territory of New Mexico first applied for admission as a free state in 1850. Unfortunately, the Civil War and its antecedent regional politics blocked our admission despite Congressman Abraham Lincoln's exhortations that we should be a free state since Spanish and Mexican law prohibited slavery".

"So why wasn't New Mexico admitted after the Civil War in 1865? Well, it seems Congress wanted more Anglos to emigrate here since we were too Hispanic in population. Congress then sped up that process by carving southern Colorado and all of Arizona from the New Mexico Territory- and admitting the Colorado territory into the Union before New Mexico".

"These actions by Congress were consistent with its refusal to fund the Surveyor General in this territory. Remember the U.S. had agreed to protect the land rights of all Hispanos residing in the new U.S. territories following the U.S.-Mexican War. But the Surveyor General had to review and approve those Spanish and Mexican land grants. Then in 1862, Congress further frustrated the process by passing a federal law shifting all the costs of land grant examination and surveying to the land grant holders. No wonder that only thirty land grants were approved by the Surveyor General out of more than sixty submitted".

"In light of this federal hostility toward us Hispanos, the success of the Alianza, under Juan's leadership, is even more remarkable. I only wish my friend Juan could hear our appreciation".

WISDOM BEGINS IN WONDER. —Socrates

CHAPTER 6
SCHOOLING TO SUCCEED

ANGELINA AND JUAN were in agreement that their three children should learn English as well as Spanish. English was to be stressed since that was the official language of the United States even though the territory of New Mexico was officially bi-lingual. All laws enacted by the territorial legislature were printed both in English and Spanish.

Angelina had been taught to read and write Spanish at home by her parents. The plan was for Angelina to learn English along with the children during Juan's evening education sessions.

In 1859, the territorial legislature directed that all settlements in the territory should have a school. The Justice of the Peace in each county was to hire a teacher and collect a fifty cent tax per child per year to support the school which would be in session from November to April.

The Justice of the Peace for their settlement of Malaga was an Anglo appointed by the county judge based in Mesilla, the county seat for Doña Ana County. Of the territory's nine counties, Doña Ana was the largest encompassing the southern one fourth of the territory from the California border on the west to the Texas border on the east. In late 1859, the western portion of Doña Ana County was severed off by Congress to form the new county of Arizona with Tucson as its county seat.

At Juan's suggestion, Alianza representatives met with the Malaga Justice of the Peace shortly after a teacher had been hired for their village. The Alianza wanted to confirm that Hispanic children could attend the school along with the Anglo children. The Justice of the Peace confirmed the legislature's open admission policy for all schools but stressed that the annual fifty cent tax per child had to be paid.

Angelina recalled that only three of the fifteen Alianza families sent their children to the Malaga school. Despite Angelina's and Juan's best efforts, many of their friends said they couldn't afford the tax while others admitted that they needed their children home to help work their farms or ranchos. Angelina was also frustrated that their daughter Maria was the only Hispanic girl to attend the school—Angelina was chided by some of the Alianza women that girls should learn cooking and other home skills, not waste their time in school.

The Buenavidas utilized Juan's few books in English in addition to his English primer from the university. They also used the periodic newspapers from St. Louis which the Butterfield stage line would leave for Juan at the Fort Stockton mercantile. The bimonthly newspaper was the family's only source of news besides travelers periodically passing through Malaga. The newspapers would be picked up by Juan or one of the Alianza members having business in Fort Stockton.

The St. Louis newspaper was how Juan learned of the Great Compromise of 1850. Juan later told his children about it during his after- dinner education sessions. "Hijos, this compromise affected us in two ways: first, the New Mexico territory's request for statehood was not approved by Congress but was deferred; second, Texas was paid by the Congress to renounce its claim for the eastern portion of New Mexico, east of the Pecos River, including our Malaga area. What I now understand is that Congress was divided over the question of slavery and whether each territory would be admitted into the Union as a free or slave state. California was admitted as a free state while Congress decided that New Mexico's citizens would decide the slavery question at the time it was admitted. The states with slaves, mostly in the south, including Texas, forced Congress to enact the Fugitive Slave Law in return for their voting to allow California to be admitted as a free state. That law requires all U.S. citizens, including us in the territories, to assist in the recovery and return of escaped slaves".

Angelina didn't understand. "Juan, why was New Mexico not admitted in 1850, either as a free or a slave state"? she asked.

"There appears to be two main reasons", replied Juan. "The newspaper says Congress couldn't agree on New Mexico's status. The anti-slavery congressmen such as Abraham Lincoln argued that New Mexico should be admitted as a free state since its Spanish and Mexican roots prohibited slavery. The pro-slavery congressmen took the position that New Mexico could not prohibit slavery. Another reason not stated in the newspaper is that as of 1850, the territory's non-Indian population was still about ninety percent Hispanic. I believe Congress was afraid to admit a territory with so many former citizens of another country, a country with which the U.S. had just fought a war. I think Congress will wait to admit New Mexico until our territory is majority Anglo".

Tomás, the eldest Buenavida child and all of nine raised his hand and asked, "Papá, what is slavery"?

Juan had paused as he decided how best to respond to his son. "Tomás, slavery is a system where a person is owned by another person, like a piece of property. In the U.S., slavery usually means an Anglo person owning a Negro person to do work on his farm".

Tomás reflected on his father's explanation and then said, "Papá, Anglos must not believe in God".

Juan had glanced at Angelina with a "Where did that statement come from" look and said, "Tomás, why do you say that"?

"Because God wants us to treat others as we want to be treated. I think treating a person as a piece of property isn't what God would want us to do", replied Tomás.

Juan and Angelina agreed but had to explain to Tomás and the other children that a majority of the Anglo slave-owners in the U.S. were Christians and the fact that they owned slaves was a contradiction that was difficult to understand.

Juan went on, "Hijos, slavery is a shameful and de-humanizing practice and most countries have abolished it. The United States still allows it even though our constitution says all men are created equal. And you should also know that Thomas Jefferson, one of the writers of the U. S. constitution and an early U.S. president, was himself a slave-owner in Virginia. It makes one wonder about hypocrisy, doesn't it, hijos"? concluded Juan.

THE BEST THING TO HOLD ON TO IN LIFE IS

EACH OTHER. —Unknown

CHAPTER 7
"EL AMOR BRUJO"
(THE BEWITCHED LOVE)

MARIA BUENAVIDA INSISTED that her mother take a nap that afternoon and rest a while from the vigil. Her father was now in day three of his coma and everyone now feared for the worse. Hadn't the doctor told the family that the sooner Juan came out of the coma the better? Her father, the grandfather of her three children, looked so much at peace as she gazed on his face. He had a full head of hair, mostly grey now but with white sideburns. Her mother combed it lovingly at least once a day as she talked to him as if he heard her softly whispered words.

As Maria sat by her parents' bed, holding her father's hand, she looked out the window and noticed a dust devil on the horizon—its spiral shape swaying sideways as tumbleweeds and dust were swept up. Suddenly, she recalled her mother telling her and her brothers a gypsy love story after dinner when they were young children. She remembered that her parents had the habit of telling them stories one night and her father teaching them English or reading from the eastern newspaper or one of his English books, the next night.

Their mother had told them about Micaela, a young and beautiful gypsy woman who had been married off to a much older man by her parents when she was quite young. The story went that Micaela had been widowed shortly after her marriage. Her husband, knowing he was dying, paid a "bad" gypsy witch to cast a spell over Micaela so that she would never love anyone. The husband did this out of spite because he knew Micaela never loved him. And so the years passed by with Micaela spurning many young mens' efforts to win her heart. It was as if Micaela didn't even see or hear the young men. Finally, a young man named Antonio fell in love with Micaela and was not dissuaded by her determined coldness. Antonio went to a "good" gypsy witch and asked for help. This good witch was told about Micaela's behavior and concluded she must be under some kind of evil spell. She recommended that Antonio have a large party attended by his men friends and Micaela's women friends—these people must be good and loyal friends, the good witch advised. At the party, Antonio was told to build a large bonfire—the larger the better. The good witch told Antonio he must obtain holy water—water blessed by a priest –and that such water must slowly be sprinkled into the fire by both Micaela and Antonio. Then the witch directed that all the friends at the party and Antonio and Micaela, must all dance around the bonfire, but only in a clockwise direction.

All the good witch's directions were carefully carried out. Maria remembered that Angelina had paused in her story telling and all the Buenavida children had cried out, "Mamá, what happened then"! Angelina had smiled at them and continued: the evil spell was broken. The good spirit of all the friends dancing rapidly around the fire plus the holy water acted as a force around the fire to suction away the evil spell holding Micaela prisoner. Immediately, Micaela's eyes and heart were opened and she saw Antonio, as if for the first time, as he held her hands as they both danced around the fire. She suddenly stopped dancing and kissed Antonio for the first time. Micaela fell in love with Antonio, they married, and lived happily ever after.

Maria smiled to herself—how curious that the now dissipated dust devil had triggered a memory from her childhood—a story of Spanish gypsies with a happy ending.

ALWAYS REMEMBER, YOU HAVE WITHIN YOU

THE STRENGTH, THE PATIENCE, AND THE PASSION

TO REACH FOR THE STARS TO CHANGE THE WORLD.

—Harriet Tubman

CHAPTER 8
AMOS

IT WAS AFTER midnight on a cool, early fall evening in 1858 when Juan was awakened by the barking of his two dogs. Unlike the usual brief one or two series of barks, this barking seemed incessant and concentrated. "Coyotes or some other predator going after our chickens", he thought as he quickly dressed and retrieved his rifle from its rack above the front door.

Outside, the cool evening air was bracing and seemed to compliment the star-filled sky. With no moon, Juan paused to allow his eyes to adjust to the darkness and shadows of trees, house, barn and animal pens and chicken coops. His two dogs were growling near the barn, not the animal pens.

Cocking his rifle, Juan slowly advanced on the barn. The barn was built with only one entrance and had no windows. Inside, the barn housed hay, the Buenavida's two milk cows and ranch equipment and tools. Juan knew that since the dogs were now growling, they had cornered something or someone, and Juan didn't think a predator would enter his closed- in barn, especially since no food was to be had there.

After swinging open the barn door, Juan shouted "Who's there"? in both English and Spanish, his back to the barn's side and his rifle ready. No response. Juan then shouted "I have a rifle and will shoot if you don't come out"!

"Mistah, don't shoot. I is coming out. I means you no harm", was the hurried response in a deep southern drawl.

"Come out slowly with your hands up so I can see them", Juan said, as he slowly looked into the barn with his rifle pointing in.

"Yessah, yessah", said a Negro man, arms up in the air, as he slowly shuffled out of the barn toward Juan.

"Stop there"! ordered Juan. "Who are you and why are you hiding in my barn"?

"I is Amos and I run away from my mastah in Texas. I want to be free man", said the Negro, his arms still held high.

Juan could see that the man was not armed except for a small metal knife with a wooden handle tucked under a rope belt around his waist. His clothes were ragged and his bare feet were bloody. He appeared to be in his early thirties. "Put you arms down and sit down over there", ordered Juan, his rifle still pointing at the Negro and indicating just inside the barn.

Juan walked sideways to the inside wall and took down a lantern which he put on the ground and quickly lit with one hand while not taking his eyes or rifle off of the now seated Negro.

"So, Amos, how long have you been running and where are you headed"? asked Juan as the lantern's light filled the front section of the barn's interior. His two dogs were at his side but had ceased their growling.

"Mistah, I leaves my cotton farm in Texas five days ago", Amos replied. "I walk west until I reached dat river and then turned north following dat river. I hears New Mexico not a slave place and dat California be a free state, but it far away to da west".

Juan sat down facing Amos, his rifle now lying across his lap. "Why did you run away, Amos"? he asked. "And you can call me Juan".

Amos bowed his head and hesitated before answering, as if he didn't know how to begin. "Mistah Juan, my owner, Mastah Jim, sold my woman after I ask him for permission to marry her. He sold her to punish Amos since Amos run away before. His whipping of Amos not enough punishment. Mastah Jim tell everybody that Amos must be made an example- the other "Niggers" need to know what happens if yous run away. I run away dat night even though they take Amos' boots away at night. But Amos fools Mastah Jim and still runs away- this time to da west and not to da south as Amos done before. Amos cuts up pants and wraps my feets- the cloth wears out two days ago. Amos walks all day and all night and not go by farmhouses". Amos paused to see if Juan had any questions. Hearing none, Amos continued. "Mistah Juan, Amos beg you let Amos stay this night in yous barn. Amos has no life now his woman been sold and gone. Amos afraid he try to kill Mastah Jim if he not runs away".

Juan felt his heart soften toward this Negro man who sat on the ground with his chin touching his chest, the bloody and muddy soles of his feet glistening in the lantern's glow. "Amos, you can stay in my barn for a few days until you get your strength back. I will get you some food and water and some boots. First we need to clean, treat and bandage your feet. Tomorrow, I need to tell my neighbors, who are all Alianza members, about you. We hear that Texan bounty hunters are being used to catch runaway slaves and we need to be ready if they show up. For that reason, Amos, you must stay inside the barn day and night. Do you understand"?

"Yessah, Mistah Juan", Amos replied, nodding his head up and down and smiling broadly. Juan told Amos he would be right back. Juan returned with a "colcha" (one of Angelina's quilts made up of different patches of fabric sewn together), some tortillas and some dried beef and water. In addition, Juan brought some cloth bandages and Angelina's salve for Amos to put on his feet after he washed them.

The next morning, Juan told Angelina, the children, and the rancho workers about Amos. He directed them not to go to the barn until he returned from advising the Alianza neighbors. As he rode over to the neighboring Martinez farm, Juan kept thinking of what he and his neighbors could do to help Amos along his journey to freedom. Juan was aware that Congress had recently passed the Fugitive Slave law that required citizens of all states to assist in the return of runaway slaves. Juan was not about to comply with what he believed to be an evil, immoral law engineered by Southern congressmen. What Amos really needed, in case he was stopped, was written proof he was a free man. Juan decided to write up and forge such a document- his conscience demanded he do all he could to help Amos.

After advising Estefan Martinez of the Amos situation, Juan rode back to Rancho Buenavida. Estefan was to advise the next Alianza neighbor and to also remind everyone to be on alert in case Texan bounty hunters arrived looking for Amos- the three shot alarm was to be sounded. Juan found Amos sitting exactly where he left him the previous night. Amos had washed and bandaged his feet and the herbal salve was visible on the bottom of his feet.

"Good morning Amos", Juan said opening the barn door. "Your feet look much better. How do you feel"?

Amos replied, "Mistah Juan, Amos feel good. Da medicine makes ma feets better".

"Good, I believe your best route is to follow the Pecos River north to Santa Rosa, and then turn west to Albuquerque or Santa Fe", Juan said. "You can find work there as I've heard that former Army Buffalo soldiers have settled in both towns. Walking thirty miles a day, it should take you ten or so days. I would like to write up a Freedman letter for you to have, just in case someone challenges you as still being a slave- we'll fold it up and have you wear it around you neck in an animal skin bag to keep it dry. After going two or three days north, I don't believe anyone from Texas will follow you. And Amos, remember that New Mexico is a free territory- plus under both the previous Spanish and Mexican governments, slavery was not allowed here. You will have to act like a free man now not a slave. Can you do that"?

Amos began to stammer- he couldn't believe what he had just heard. This Hispanic rancher who spoke English had just given Amos a plan for his freedom. And to be given a writing saying he was a free man- Amos was incredulous. "Mistah Juan", Amos said, almost choking on his words, "Amos thank you for saving Amos. You be the first person to help Amos his whole life".

That night, based on the general information provided by Amos, Juan and Angelina wrote up the following on good parchment paper:

Notice to All

For good service rendered, this Negro man of 31 years by the name of Amos was given his freedom on August 1ˢᵗ, 1858 by his owner James Martin of the J and J Farm, Little Springs, Texas.

(Signature) James Martin

The next morning Amos left the Buenavida rancho and began walking north, along the west side of the Pecos River. A pair of Juan's used boots on his feet and wearing some of Juan's clothes, Amos had a large cloth sack with beef jerky and tortillas prepared by Angelina on his back. On his side, he carried an animal skin water bag. Tied around his neck, in an animal skin bag, was his freedman paper.

Juan later told Angelina and their children how he had seen the keloid scars criss-crossed on Amos' back when he was putting on the clothes Juan had given him. Those scars confirmed Amos' account of being repeatedly whipped and beaten by his Texas slaveowner. Angelina said "Que Dios lo bendiga" (May God bless him) and expressed her feelings that whatever was in Amos' future, it had to be better than his past.

LIFE IS A JOURNEY, NOT A DESTINATION. —Unknown

CHAPTER 9
RECOLLECTIONS OF A
CHILDHOOD

IT WAS DAY four of his father's coma. Tomás Buenavida and his wife were sitting in his parents' bedroom among family members and many neighbors and friends. The smells of votive candles and the menthyladum his mother had applied on his father's chest filled the room. Tomás, his brother Marcos, his sister Maria, and their mother had rotated the vigil duty of sitting alongside the bed, holding their father's hand and occasionally wiping his brow with a wet hand towel.

Tomás had just completed his three hour shift and walked out to the front porch of his parents' home. He needed the fresh air and the freedom to lose himself in the colorful majesty of the New Mexico sunset. From inside, the yellow and then orange hues had colored the bedroom windows. Now, leaning against one of the portal's (porch) support columns, Tomás gazed to his right and soaked in the reds and purples of the waning sunset over the Guadalupe Mountains to the west.

Tomás just couldn't believe his father was there inside, in a coma, and probably dying. His earliest memory of his father was one where he was on horseback sitting in front of his father as they rode on the Buenavida Rancho. He remembered feeling frightened because he was so high up off the ground, but yet feeling safe with his father's left arm around him. He recalled feeling that he, his father, and the horse were all one entity, moving with a rhythmic, bouncing gait around the ranch. Later, Tomás recalled his father's story of how Montezuma and his Aztec priests, who had never seen a horse, had viewed the invading Spanish conquistadores and their horses as one being, one God. No wonder Cortez and his small army conquered such a vast empire so easily. The fact that Cortez was red haired also had helped because the Aztecs had previously been visited by friendly red- haired travelers who had promised to return – the Aztec priests had counseled Montezuma that the Spaniards might be related to those earlier visitors.

Growing up on the Buenavida Ranch involved much hard work for Tomás and his siblings. His father and mother both expected the children to do their chores and their duties increased commensurate with their ages and abilities. For Tomás, that progression went from gathering eggs from the chicken coop, feeding, and watering the livestock, cleaning out the horse stalls, and then helping lead cattle and mend fences and corrals. The work had been hard, but everyone worked hard.

Thinking back, Tomás recalled how he looked forward to the post dinner evenings. Everyone had helped wash, dry, and put away the dinner dishes and pots and pans. Then it was either story-telling time with his father and mother alternating, or it was education time with his father reading from the family Bible, the eastern newspapers or from his favorite book, <u>Don Quixote</u>. Later, when the Buenavida children were in school, those education nights also involved homework and textbook reviews.

His father's reading's from <u>Don Quixote</u> were Tomás' favorite nights. His father had explained that Cervantes' story was actually a satire of the Spanish conquistadors and their exploitation of the "New World". Cortez and many of his fellow conquistadores had grown up in the Extremadura region of Spain- an impoverished, semi-arid region providing no future or success for anyone but the rich or nobility. Don Quixote's tilting at windmills as an old knight provided a contrast to the young, poor Spaniard conquistadores striking it rich at the expense of the Indians in the Americas. And as the riches returned to the Motherland, the conquistadores were rewarded with titles of nobility and royal grants of land in the new world.

YOU DO NOT GO BACK TO THE ORIGINAL PROPRIETOR.

YOU NEED A BILL OF SALE FROM GOD ALMIGHTY.

—Judge Theophilus Harrington, in a Vermont case, refusing to
turn over a slave to a plaintiff who claimed ownership under the
Fugitive Slave Act. See Russell, Supreme Court of Vermont, 6
Green Bag 77(1894)

CHAPTER 10
TEXAN BOUNTY HUNTERS

TWO DAYS AFTER Amos' departure, the Alianza's alarm system had its first test when Savino Urquidez fired three shots in quick succession. When Juan and five other Alianza neighbors galloped to the Urquidez farm they found a standoff between four armed Anglo Texans and Savino and his two workers. The Alianza members quickly dismounted behind Savino, their rifles at their sides. Juan quickly learned from Savino in Spanish that the Texans demanded to search Savino's property to see if he was hiding a runaway slave. Savino had refused.

Juan addressed the four dust- covered and sweaty Texans, who were still mounted with their hands on their revolvers, in English:

"Señores, my name is Juan Buenavida and I am the head of the Rio Pecos Alianza. I count nine guns on our side versus four of you. That dust on the horizon means more of our Alianza members are riding here as I speak. Unless you are U.S. Marshalls with a valid search warrant, we will not allow you to search any of our homes or buildings for any reason".

The oldest of the four Texans took a long hard look at Juan and said, "We are not U.S. Marshalls, but we have a right under the federal Fugitive Slave Law to find and take back to Texas any runaway slaves. We're looking for a nigger male about six foot tall and about thirty years old, called Amos. Have you or any of your Alianza members seen him"?

Juan stepped forward, narrowing the twenty feet gulf between the Texans and the Alianza members and replied, "Señor, this land is part of the Territory of New Mexico, a free territory. It is not Texas. We have not seen any runaway slaves. I think it would be best for you and your men to turn around and ride back to Texas".

The Texans looked at their leader and at Juan and the Alianza members. Juan could almost read their thoughts- is one slave worth us being shot by these armed and organized Hispanics? The leader glared at Juan, removed his hand from his revolver and turned his horse around. The other Texans followed suit and they all rode away, heading southeast, toward the Pecos River and toward Texas.

Juan gathered the Alianza men around him. "I think it's best if we all follow the Texans at a safe distance. We need to make certain they cross the Pecos and do head back to Texas. If they swing around north before the river, we'll sound the alarm and confront them again. We have all heard stories about these Texans being vicious and careless bounty hunters. Remember that compadre who rode through here from Chihuahua a few weeks ago- he told us about Texans going into Mexico and killing peaceful Yaqui Indians because the Mexican Army federales were paying a silver peso for each Apache Indian scalp brought in. The federales didn't know the scalps weren't from Apaches. Imagine killing and scalping innocent Indian women and children for a peso".

Since the Pecos was so close, the Alianza members were soon able to confirm the four Texans had crossed the river and were headed southeast. They watched until the riders and their dust disappeared over the horizon.

WORRY IS THE RUST OF THE SOUL.

—Carlos Ruiz Zafon, <u>The Shadow of the Wind</u>

CHAPTER 11
MONTEZUMA'S REVENGE

ANGELINA REFUSED TO believe that Juan would not come out of his coma. After four days of nonstop praying to her Virgen de Guadalupe, Angelina saw no change in Juan's condition. How long can someone live without food and water? Their friends and neighbors still came to pay their respects and join in the vigil. Everyone brought food so that Angelina and the Buenavidas could be spared cooking for everyone- the large kitchen table hosted a never ending assortment of fried chicken, chili stews, beans, potato dishes, tortillas, vegetables, and roast beef. Coffee pots on the wood stove continuously emitted their earthy aroma in the kitchen.

Angelina was now accustomed to the routine: the visitors would seek her out, inquire of any changes and then they would claim an empty chair in the bedroom where their rosaries would emerge. Angelina, a devout Catholic, wondered how God was reacting to the hundreds of prayers being directed his way on Juan's behalf- she had been taught that one single prayer was sufficient to get God's attention. If it was HIS will. As she sat next to the bed holding Juan's hand, she glanced at their friends and neighbors seated around the room- maybe it was God's will not to revive Juan. She shuddered at this thought and decided to reflect back on their life together- something humorous to snap her away from such pessimism and her doubting God's love.

Angelina recalled one of their education nights when their children were in their early teens. Juan had surprised them all by asking, "Who knows what 'Montezuma's Revenge' is"? Tomás had volunteered that he had heard it dealt with people getting sick while visiting in Mexico. Juan had said yes, that was part of it.

Juan then had explained that the "revenge" was Montezuma's for the Spanish conquest of Mexico- a bloody rape of a Stone Age culture overseen by condoning priests preoccupied with destroying Aztec culture and its religion. The Aztecs had a food unknown to the Spaniards: chile. Not only was it spicy hot to the taste, it universally caused a painful diahhria among the Europeans. Although not fatal as the new diseases the Spanish brought with them and their devastating effect on the indigenous peoples, the new world chile still wreaked digestive havoc on the conquerors. "Not only was it hot going down, it was hot coming out", Juan had added to everyone's laughter.

Juan had continued by stating that there was another definition to "Montezuma's Revenge". Another food of the Aztecs new to the Spaniards was corn. The Spaniards loved it fresh and also dried and ground up into tortillas. And so they brought it back to Spain as dried corn kernels or cobs - the most convenient shipping form. Unfortunately, the Spaniards did not know that the raw dried corn had to be cured with a caustic before it should be consumed. Eating uncured dried corn caused constipation and even death among the Europeans. "Montezuma must have smiled from the grave", Juan had added.

"The other new world food the Spanish found was the turkey", Juan continued. "The Aztecs had domesticated the turkey and in fact, used turkey meat in their tamales. The turkey proved to be so popular in Spain that the king ordered each returning ship to bring back at least four live turkeys."

IF YOU CAN MEET WITH TRIUMPH AND DISASTER AND

TREAT THOSE TWO IMPOSTORS JUST THE SAME.

—Rudyard Kipling

CHAPTER 12
SOME NEW MEXICO HISTORY

NEAR HIS PARENTS' bed, Marcos Buenavida sat holding his father's large and rough hand. He was the fourth in the vigil rotation- after his mother, his brother and sister. Despite the solemnity of his father's coma, Marcos smiled inwardly. "Soy el ultimo otra vez" (I am the last again), he said to himself.

As the youngest child, Marcos always felt he was trying to catch up with his two older siblings- it seemed to him that the rites of passage on the Buenavida Rancho arrived for him at a glacial pace. Even the various daily chores for the children were doled out to him long after he believed he was capable of performing them. This sense of frustration instilled in Marcos a determination to excel in everything- he would show them that they had been wrong to hold him back.

As he had ridden to his parent's home, Marcos thought about his childhood. Now fifty-six years old, he reflected on all that his parents had accomplished. The Buenavida Rancho was perfectly located- west of the Pecos River and just north of its confluence with the smaller Black River flowing from the west. The original herd of cattle his father and his family had driven from their former rancho had grown substantially, despite the annual sale of cattle to the U.S. Army garrisons at Fort Stockton to the south or Fort Sumner to the north. The original one hundred sixty acre homestead his parents patented had been subdivided to him and his siblings. The cattle and alfalfa fields he rode by had sustained the Buenavidas all these decades. In the distance, Marcos caught sight of Rancho Buenavida- his parents' home. The original adobe house had been expanded, with rooms added on either side. The large "portal" with its territorial architectural style columns in front of the entire house was now dwarfed by the tall, white- barked cottonwood trees surrounding the home on all sides.

Marcos recalled how, as a child, he had looked on his father as the smartest man on earth. The education sessions after dinner with his father enthralling the family with stories and histories- yes, those were the best of times. Marcos especially enjoyed his father's telling them of New Mexico's history. Marcos would sit on the floor, near his father and tried to write down on his school tablet the key points. Marcos still remembered the evening when he learned of the first three capitals of the royal province of New Spain in New Mexico. Spain managed its New World colonies through four viceroyalties- the viceroyalty of New Spain headquartered in Mexico City and governing North America and three other viceroyalties governing Central and South America. His father had drawn them a map showing the Americas divided up into those viceroyalties.

It had been Governor Juan de Oñate in 1598 that established the first capitol of San Juan de los Caballeros just north of present day Española. After a battle with Pueblo Indians at Acoma, Oñate relocated the capitol to San Gabriel, at the confluence of the Rio Grande and the Chama Rivers in 1600. Due to Indian pressures, San Gabriel was deserted within a year. In 1608, Oñate was removed as Governor and recalled to Mexico City to be tried for mistreatment of the Indians. In 1608, a new governor, Pedro de Peralta, established the new capitol at Santa Fe with additional colonists from Spain and Mexico. For seventy years the Spanish colony at Santa Fe thrived until 1680 when the Pueblo Indians revolted and drove the Spanish south. It was not until 1692, twelve years later, that Don Diego de Vargas recolonized Santa Fe.

It would then be one hundred fifty years later that New Mexico would face a new enemy, Anglos from the east. Juan had explained that in 1803 France had sold the U.S. the "Louisiana Purchase", over 600 million acres of land from Louisiana and the Mississippi River to the Rocky Mountains, doubling the size of the United States for $15 million. This sale, Juan explained, made the United States an immediate neighbor to Spain's territory in North America.

Then, in 1841, Texas soldiers invaded New Mexico and claimed all its land east of the Rio Grande. Governor Manuel Armijo and Hispanic volunteer soldiers quickly repulsed the Texans. In 1846, the United States declared war against Mexico. And coincidentally, U.S. General Stephen Watts Kearny and his army also arrived in Santa Fe in 1846 and "annexed" New Mexico to the United States. Two years later, the Treaty of Guadalupe Hidalgo ended the U.S.-Mexican War in 1848, with Mexico ceding all its southwestern and western lands to the United States.

Marcos remembered asking his father what Mexico had done to bring on this war with the U.S. His father had explained that that war was a war of opportunity- the U.S. was eager to acquire Mexico's lands to fulfill its "manifest destiny"-enlarging the United States from the Atlantic ocean to the Pacific. His father had explained that many in Congress had opposed the war with Mexico as being "immoral", "a land grab", and "not justified". Marcos had a difficult time squaring what he heard about the U.S.'s motives with what he was learning at school about the "land of the free" and "justice for all".

Juan then had told his children that in 1854, the U.S. had purchased from Mexico thirty thousand square miles in northern Mexico that gave the territory the bootheel of southwestern New Mexico and a strip of land south of the New Mexico territory which later became part of Arizona. The sale had been suggested by the Mexican dictator, General Santa Ana (of the Alamo fame). It seemed the General needed the money to pay his Army and refill his coffers. The newspapers said that the United States accomplished two objectives with this purchase-first, it settled the festering dispute with Mexico over the exact location of the border between the two countries and second, the United States acquired the land it needed for a southern railroad route. Juan had explained that this sale, known as the "Gadsen Purchase", was widely unpopular and criticized in Mexico. It was seen as another United States intrusion into Mexico's sovereignty.

HOPE IS THE THING WITH FEATHERS

THAT PERCHES IN THE SOUL.

—Emily Dickinson

CHAPTER 13
"EL CAMPOSANTO"

ON A SMALL hill a short walk west from the main house, the Buenavidas had established a family camposanto (cemetery). Surrounded by a low rock-pile fence, it was shadowed by a large cottonwood tree. Angelina walked there after completing her turn at her husband's vigil. She needed to get away from the house. Her Juan had built a small wooden bench within the cemetery. The family cemetery contained only two small gravestones.

Angelina sat on the shaded bench and gazed upon the two gravestones- one read "Lucia Chavez Buenavida", Juan's mother who had passed away in 1891; the other was for her second child, Eduardo, who died in 1853, having lived only two months. Angelina's eyes began to tear- even after almost 60 years; she still felt the same pain, like a sudden emptiness in her soul. Only mothers must experience this, she thought. To conceive a child, have it grow within you for nine months, endure the pain of childbirth, and be handed the crying newborn to suckle- how can anyone, other than another mother understand the bond that develops with a new born baby? And then to lose the baby so suddenly – it had been as if a part of her being had been amputated. Angelina had gone on with her life after Eduardo's death, but it was a life with a permanent void. It was as if the amputated piece of her had left a throbbing scar. The fact that most of the Hispanic families she knew in the area had lost at least one child shortly after birth didn't lessen the pain Angelina felt.

Angelina came to the "camposanto" to talk with Lucia- she had loved her mother-in-law due to her kindness and her unconditional acceptance of Angelina into the Buenavida family. Angelina's mother had died shortly after Angelina had married Juan and Lucia had, in effect, become her mother. Lucia had taught her all that she knew about managing a household, cooking, herbs, home remedies and how to be a matriarch. Lucia, especially in her later years, had developed a reputation of being an effective "curandera" (healer) and Angelina had learned much about the healing arts by assisting her.

Living in the Buenavida household, Angelina had had many "soul to soul" talks with Lucia. Lucia had always managed to offer kind advice without a condescending or superior attitude. Angelina missed her deeply.

A slight afternoon breeze had picked up and the cottonwood tree and its leaves rustled softly above her. Angelina again focused on Lucia's gravestone. "Lucia, please intercede with the Virgen, Jesus, and all the saints on behalf of your son and my husband", she prayed. Angelina knew Lucia was in heaven since she had been such a good person. Lucia would help save her Juan- a miracle was needed so that Juan would recover from his coma. Angelina closed her eyes, bowed her head and softly prayed ten Hail Marys.

Just as Angelina concluded the last prayer, she heard "Lina, no te vayas de Dios" (don't remove yourself from God) in a soft voice. Angelina froze, her head still bowed. Only Lucia had called her Lina. Was Lucia talking to her from heaven? Another gust of wind suddenly swept through the large cottonwood tree. Is that what Angelina had heard? Or were those the words she wanted to hear? She slowly raised her head and stared at Lucia's gravestone.

"No, Lucia, I will not stray from God", she said. Angelina had to answer the admonition she thought she had heard. Angelina knew only God could save Juan. She stood and slowly walked back to her home.

IT IS THE TRIUMPH OF REASON TO GET ON WELL WITH THOSE WHO POSSESS NONE. —Voltaire

CHAPTER 14
FOR WHOM DOES
"LA LLORONA" CRY?

MARIA BUENAVIDA SAT along her parents' bedroom wall waiting for her turn to sit alongside her father. In the quiet of the late afternoon, her two elderly paternal aunts were softly crying in a corner. Their brother's continued coma was finally manifesting itself as despair.

As Maria heard the soft crying and felt her aunts' anguish, she was reminded of her grandmother Lucia Buenavida's "La Llorona" (The Crier) stories. Maria had been only five or six years old the first time her grandmother had scared her silly with the story. Maria remembered it had been a nighttime story-telling sometime close to El Dia De Los Muertos (the Day of the Dead) in early November. Grandmother Buenavida had previously explained to her grandchildren about the Aztec celebration honoring all deceased family members. The Aztecs believed that death was not the end of life; it was just one of life's many stages. El Dia De Los Muertos was the ultimate family reunion. All of your ancestors come back on November first and second and the family prepares meals and a party for them. Her grandmother had explained that the Buenavidas didn't celebrate the holiday, but many of their neighbors did.

Maria had sat between her two brothers at their grandmother's feet that evening. Just recalling that first time caused Maria to shiver. Grandmother Buenavida had started by warning the three children not to walk near the river or acequias (ditches) at night because they might hear a young woman crying and if they did hear the pitiful wailing, they had to run home as fast as they could. Maria had asked her grandmother why they had to run and why shouldn't they stay and try to help the woman.

"Mija", her grandmother had replied, "you must hear the story of La Llorona and then you will understand."

"A long time ago, in a small town not too far from here, there lived a very beautiful girl. Although her parents were poor farmers, they hoped that their daughter's beauty would allow her to marry a rich young man. And in fact, the son of the richest family in the town asked permission to court her. Of course, her parents consented. The two soon fell in love and became lovers. The girl became pregnant and the young man, clearly overjoyed, told the girl and her parents that he would marry her. However, his parents flatly refused to allow the marriage- telling the son that the girl was beneath their class and unacceptable, pregnant or not. And to prevent their son eloping with the girl, his parents quickly arranged a marriage for their son with the daughter of another rich family. The son at first refused to comply, but had to relent when threatened with being disinherited. The poor girl was heartbroken and her parents were devastated. A few months later, the girl delivered twins- a beautiful and healthy girl and boy. No other young man came forward to court the young mother and her babies.

Two years passed and it became clear that the rich young man and his rich wife could not have any children.

"Then the Devil and his evil ways appeared. The parents of the rich young man invited the poor girl's parents to their hacienda. They shamelessly offered the poor farmer and his wife a large sum of money for their two grandchildren saying the children would have a better life with them and their father. The farmer, over the objection of his wife, accepted the proposal, saying he would bring the children the next day. The young poor girl soon learned of her father's action when she questioned her crying mother. Her father explained that this arrangement would help her find a husband since she would no longer be hindered by two children. Besides, the farmer continued, the children would be brought up by their father and have a good life. We can barely feed ourselves now he said, his head bowed with guilt as his daughter began to cry.

" That night, after her parents were asleep, the young girl quietly took her two sleeping children out of the small farmhouse. She softly cried as she walked to the nearby river where she quickly submerged and drowned first one and then the other of her sleeping babies. After laying their limp little bodies on the river's bank the young girl walked back into the river holding two large rocks in her arms. She walked until the cold water covered her head and then sat down, tightly clutching the rocks. The next morning, the farmer and the town folks discovered the three bodies.

"So, mijos, La Llorona is the ghost of that sad young mother. Many people say she is crying because she drowned her two babies. Others say she is crying because her lover betrayed her; still others say she is crying because her own parents betrayed her. Regardless, most of us believe she walks along the rivers and acequias trying to replace her two dead children. But in her soul she knows she is doing wrong by trying to kidnap young children. So, she loudly cries and wails as she walks at night in order to warn all the children that she is approaching".

Maria remembered she had had nightmares about the sad La Llorona for weeks after hearing her grandmother's story. But, Maria also knew she would never allow herself or her children near the rivers or acequias at night.

NOTHING IS WORTH MORE THAN THIS DAY. —Unknown

CHAPTER 15
A BRITISH BATH

THE BUENAVIDA KITCHEN was always a source of warm recollections for Marcos Buenavida. As the youngest of the three Buenavida children, Marcos grew up with the kitchen's fragrant smells of the frijoles (bean) pot, the unique spicy aroma of green chile being roasted, and his mother's flour tortillas – hot from the stove and delicious with the churned butter.

Now fifty-six years old, Marcos sat at his parents' family kitchen table. Shorter than his brother Tomás, he was clearly graying and felt exhausted. He had just completed his turn at his father's bedside. And while the kitchen was alive with relatives, friends and neighbors preparing, bringing and eating food, Marcos just wanted to eat a quick snack and ride home.

Their father had given Tomás and Marcos each forty acres of the one hundred sixty acre homestead upon their respective marriages. He had always told his sons that since they had helped work the ranch, they should share in the land. Tomás, having married first, chose the southwestern quadrant along the Rio Negro and Marcos had selected the northeastern quadrant along the Pecos River.

Riding home in the late autumn afternoon, Marcos forced himself to think about anything other than his father's coma or his mother's deepening despair. Marcos decided to recall his family's after- dinner education sessions. Besides his father's readings from Don Quixote, the eastern newspapers, or books in English, occasionally their parents would ask if the children had any questions. Marcos remembered the night he had asked his first question. It had been when he was in the sixth grade, in 1866.

His school teacher, Mrs. McAllister had told the class that June was the traditional wedding month. Marcos hadn't understood why a certain month was so designated, but was afraid to ask the teacher to explain. So, he quickly had raised his hand and asked his father and mother that night. He recalled his father had laughed at the question, but congratulated Marcos for asking his first family question.

"Hijo", his father had said, "I am not laughing at you, but only remembering something I learned at university in Mexico City. My English literature professor was British and he was a very funny professor. It was he who explained English history and customs so I can answer your question. In the 1500's in England, the average person had only one yearly bath in May. Can you imagine that? What do you think they smelled like before that annual bath? - Ay Dios! So people in England got married in June because they still smelled pretty good from their recent bath. However, since they were starting to smell, English brides carried a bouquet of very fragrant flowers, called "nosegay" by the English, to help mask their body odor. That custom of the bride carrying a bouquet is still followed today here in the United States, even though fortunately, people do now take more frequent baths"!

Marcos remembered that everyone had laughed in amazement at their papá's explanation. But, his papá wasn't finished.

"The professor also told us that those annual baths occurred in one big wooden tub filled with boiled water. The man of the house had the privilege of bathing first in the nice clean water, then all the sons and other men, then the women and finally the children. The last to be bathed were the babies. By then the bath water was so dirty and dark, you could actually lose someone in it. Hence, the English saying- 'Don't throw the baby out with the bath water"!

Marcos recalled that he and his siblings had reacted in shock at their papá's account. How disgusting a practice! And to think that the United States was so proud of its English roots- at least in the East.

Marcos rode on with a smile on his face. He had to tell his children about their grandfather's story.

MAY YOU WALK GENTLY THROUGH THE WORLD AND

KNOW ITS BEAUTY ALL THE DAYS OF YOUR LIFE.

—Apache Blessing

CHAPTER 16
THE CATTLE DRIVE

HIS FATHER'S VIGIL was now probably very similar to the English wakes of the 1500's his father had told them about as children, thought Tomás. The English then had not learned from the Romans and still imbibed their liquor from lead and pewter cups. Since the liquor's alcohol leached out the lead from the cups, the combination of the alcohol and lead caused the drinker to pass out for days. So the English "wakes" involved the families waiting for the laid out relative to wake up, or not.

Tomás was sitting along one of the walls in his parents' bedroom. Across the room, several family members were quietly praying the rosary. The Virgen de Guadalupe velas (candles) on the bedroom's dresser were ablaze with light in the late afternoon shadows. The mirror above the dresser further reflected the light from the velas onto the bedroom's ceiling, making it come alive.

Antonio Muñoz, one of his father's best friends and fellow cattle rancher, was sitting nearby and spoke up during a lapse in the conversation. "Tomás, do you remember our cattle drive to Fort Sumner in 1865"?

Tomás smiled and responded, "Yes, Don Antonio, it was my first and at the age of 13 that cattle drive made many good memories. My father had learned that the United States Army at Fort Sumner was buying cattle plus Fort Sumner was paying a higher price than what Fort Stockton to the south was paying. You and my father decided to drive one hundred head along the west side of the Pecos all the way to Fort Sumner. Due to the proximity of the river, you both calculated that we could drive the cattle 30 miles a day and reach Fort Sumner in five days".

"Tomás, your memory is very good", Don Antonio interjected. "I remember you and another rider bringing up the rear and rounding up the strays. You all had to wear bandanas over your faces because of the dust kicked up by the cattle. What do you remember most about that cattle drive"?

"Don Antonio, what I remember most were those poor Indians we saw at the Bosque Redondo near Fort Sumner", replied Tomás. "The Army had eight thousand or so Navajos living next to five hundred or so Mescalero Apaches- their long time enemies. We learned from the Army quartermaster who paid for the cattle that Colonel Kit Carson and his soldiers had forcibly captured and marched these Indians thought to be "hostile" from their homelands all the way to the Bosque Redondo in northeastern New Mexico. The Apaches were first in 1863 and the Navajos were forced on their "long walk" there in 1864. We also learned that the Army at Fort Sumner had planned only for 5,000 Indians, not the 8,500 brought there. Fighting broke out often between the Apaches and the Navajos. Besides the poor and inconsistent corn crops, the bad water, the Army had to bring in fire wood from Santa Rosa to the north. Many of these "hostile" Indians died during this punishment experiment by the Army which didn't include the peaceful Pueblo Indians of northern New Mexico".

"Yes, those Indians were living in terrible, pitiful conditions and the Army had its hands full just keeping them contained", said Don Antonio as he slowly shook his head remembering while looking down at his boots. "In fact, we learned later that the Mescalero Apaches escaped from the Bosque in 1865, but the Navajos were not allowed to return to their home area in northwestern New Mexico, then officially a reservation, until 1868".

"Yes, Don Antonio", replied Tomás, "I remember my father reading to us from several newspapers he regularly received from the Butterfield stage stop of Fort Stockton. Those eastern newspaper stories described U.S. Army Indian policy ranging from outright extermination, forcible relocation as punishment such as we saw at Bosque Redondo, to beneficial protectionism. Those newspaper stories also revealed that the costs in assigned troops and money were high, regardless of which Indian policy was implemented. Unfortunately, the impact on the Indians was severe. We later learned that thousands of Indians died at Bosque Redondo from starvation and illness and from the long marches from and back to their homelands".

"What we also learned from the newspapers was that the United States had promised Mexico in the Treaty of Guadalupe Hildalgo that it would stop Apache attacks into Mexico. Even after allocating sixty percent of all of its Army soldiers to the southwestern border, the United States still was not able to comply with its treaty obligation. Mexico protested and filed a 20 to 30 million dollar claim against the United States for its losses due to the continuing Indian attacks".

"I guess it wasn't until Geronimo surrendered in 1886 that Indian hostilities in the southwest finally ended", added Don Antonio. "I personally don't blame the Indians for resenting the Anglos. They took their lands and killed them if they resisted and then broke peace treaties repeatedly as Anglo settlers continued to push west. Many tribes were relocated several times to increasingly desolate reservations. No wonder some Indian tribes fought back. You know Tomás, you only need to look at what the peaceful Taos Pueblo Indians did to New Mexico's first Anglo territorial governor, Charles Bent in 1847. They killed and scalped him at his Taos home. It took 200 soldiers from Fort Union in Las Vegas to put down the Hispano and Indian revolt against U.S. rule. The change from Spanish and Mexican rule to Anglo U.S. rule apparently had a harsh impact especially on the Indian peoples".

"I agree Don Antonio," added Tomás. "There is a fundamental difference in how the Spanish and Mexican settlers interacted with the Indian populations in New Mexico with the Anglo experience in general. Many Navajos, Apaches, and Pueblo Indians have Spanish surnames as a result of intermarrying with Hispanos. Contrast that to the Anglo Indian experience in the eastern United States- most eastern Indian tribes were annihilated or relocated westward, like the Seminoles of Florida. And U.S. peace treaties with the Indians were not honored. Spain, on the other hand did generally honor them, like the one that Spanish Governor Juan Bautista de Anza brokered with the Comanches in 1786— that treaty ended the Comanche raids against New Mexico's Hispano settlements and Pueblo Indians. United States Indian policy seemed to be based on an institutional Anglo prejudice against anyone not Anglo, I think. The same prejudice was and is still being practiced by Anglos against Negroes and us Hispanos".

"Well Tomás, we've drifted a bit from the nostalgia of your first cattle drive", said Don Antonio, as he stood up to leave. Tomás stood also and helped his father's elderly compadre to the front door.

LIFE IS TOO SHORT TO WASTE HATING ANYONE.

—Unknown

CHAPTER 17
THE CONFEDERATE
INVASION

MARIA SAT ALONE at the large kitchen table of her parent's home. She had just completed her vigil turn by her father's bedside. The hot cup of coffee she was enjoying before leaving for her home was having the desired effect. With each passing day, Maria was noticing her Mother's decline- how could she help her mother get through this if her father didn't come out of his coma?

Maria forced herself to think about anything else. On the wall across from the kitchen table was the yellowed St. Louis newspaper article her father had placed in a frame. "CIVIL WAR ENDS!" it shouted. Maria closed her eyes and remembered back to 1865 when she had been just ten years old. Her father had gathered everyone after dinner to explain the war's impact on the New Mexico territory.

Her father had explained the Confederate strategy involving New Mexico he had read about in the St. Louis newspaper. The Confederates had planned to establish a southwestern Confederate state comprised of southern portions of New Mexico and Arizona with its capitol at Mesilla, New Mexico. The Confederate grand scheme was to seize the silver and gold mines of New Mexico, Arizona, and California and eventually the sea ports of southern California. Her father explained that in 1862 the Confederates were very nearly successful. A Confederate Army from Texas had won battles at Mesilla and Albuquerque and then had captured Santa Fe.

The Union forces from Santa Fe had retreated to Fort Union in Las Vegas- the last remaining Union fort in the territory. The Union forces were comprised of units of the Colorado Infantry, the U.S. Calvary, the U.S. Infantry and the New Mexico militia. Many members of the New Mexico militia were Hispanos and Pueblo Indians- they were lead by a Lt. Colonel Manual Chaves. Many Hispanos had eagerly joined the militia due to their hatred of Texans. Maria remembered someone asking her father why Texans were so disliked. He had explained that many factors created that sentiment: the many raids by Texans into southern New Mexico, the Texas Republic's claim to all of New Mexico east of the Rio Grande, the state of Texas allowing slavery, and the many reports of anti-Hispanic incidents in Texas.

Her father had explained that Glorieta Pass was the only pass through the Sangre de Cristo Mountains that run north and south between Santa Fe and Las Vegas. The Santa Fe Trail used this pass. The battle of Glorieta Pass proved to be the turning point of the civil war in New Mexico because, while the 2 day battle was a stalemate, the New Mexico militia found, destroyed and burned the Confederate supply train to the rear of the Confederate army. Without their supplies and replacement horses, the Confederates were forced to retreat to Texas.

As a result, New Mexico had not become a Confederate state. Her father had stressed how they should all be proud of those volunteer Hispano and Pueblo Indian militia members- farmers and ranchers like themselves- who were instrumental in defeating the Confederate enemy.

LIVE DELIBERATELY, TO FRONT ONLY THE ESSENTIAL

FACTS OF LIFE. —Henry David Thoreau

CHAPTER 18
THE SANTA FE TRIP

ANGELINA'S BLACK DRESS she had made herself. She decided to wear it daily at the vigil as many of the women coming to pay their respects were dressed in black.

Angelina recalled that the dress fabric had been purchased when Juan and ten other Alianza members decided to travel to Santa Fe in August, 1855. Juan had learned that the U.S. Congress in 1854 had passed a law granting to each resident who resided in the New Mexico territory before 1853, a donation of 160 acres if the land was occupied and worked for at least four years. The men wanted to go and file their 160 acre donation claims or to submit proof of their Spanish or Mexican land grants with the recently appointed U.S. Surveyor General in Santa Fe.

Before departing, Juan had convened an Alianza meeting at Rancho Buenavida. He had explained that the U.S. Congress was paying the salaries of the territorial governor, legislature and the Surveyor General. Juan was concerned that Congress would be influenced to not adequately fund the work of the Surveyor General. Some disreputable

Anglo land speculators, it seemed, wanted to delay approvals of land grants in the territory with the hope of obtaining these lands cheaply or by force. Some at the meeting raised the point that the Treaty of Guadalupe Hidalgo required the United States and its Congress to honor those Spanish and Mexican land grants. Juan had replied that treaties, like any law, have to be enforced or they are just so many words on paper. Mexico was in no position to force U.S. compliance with the treaty- especially on behalf of its former citizens. Juan explained that the Alianza members needed to act quickly now that the Surveyor General had finally been appointed – five years late. The 1854 law required that the 160 acre donation claims be filed with the Surveyor General as soon as possible with the ownership rights patented after proof of the four years of occupation and use. Juan recommended that all the Alianza members without land grants file their claims for the 160 acre donations. He also stated that the Alianza members needed to pool their money in case an attorney needed to be hired in Santa Fe to help process their claims.

Angelina had volunteered to canvass the Alianza women to determine what supplies could be purchased in Santa Fe. Everyone knew that the Santa Fe Trail wagon trains from Missouri arrived in Santa Fe each year in early August. The U.S. made products, especially the fabrics and manufactured goods were very desirable. Products from Mexico were also available in Santa Fe having been brought north along the Chihuahua trail. The products from the East were usually much better quality than the products from Mexico. If enough supplies were to be ordered, the Alianza men would have to take along a wagon, as pack horses would not be sufficient. Angelina had ordered dress fabric and thread for her and Maria – including the black dress fabric.

Upon their return, Juan had described the group's meeting with the Surveyor General, an Anglo. He accepted all their claims for the 160 acre donations, but stated that each claim had to be surveyed by the claimant. Final patents could be requested after four years of proven use and occupation. He was less welcoming of the Alianza members with land grants. Besides having to incur the costs of surveying their lands, he stated that his office had few resources to evaluate the validity of the land grants, be they Spanish or Mexican in origin. He expressed frustration in not having been given procedures by Congress for assessing the validity of such land grants. When pressed by Juan, the Surveyor General admitted his office did not have any resources to offer any assistance to land grant claimants and also could not predict the timeframe for review or approval. Dismayed, the Alianza group decided to hire an attorney. The only Hispanic attorney in the city, an Alberto Gonzales, met with the Alianza members and agreed to represent them. He was already representing other Hispano land grant claimants in the territory.

Juan had also told Angelina that he had been quite impressed with Santa Fe. Its adobe buildings surrounded the town's plaza with the Palace of the Spanish Governors forming the north side. The United States Fort Marcy was located to the north of the plaza while many mercantile shops filled in. The town's small streets were not laid out in a grid, but followed what must have been former burro trails. The aromatic smells of piñon wood cookfires had filled the valley in which Santa Fe lay surrounded by mountains on three sides.

In retrospect, the Alianza claimants had been largely successful in obtaining patents for their 160 acre claims. It had taken more than three years after the four years of use Congress had specified. Congress, however, continued to delay and frustrate any process to adjudicate land grant claims. Less than half of all land grant claims were approved by the Surveyors General of the various southwestern states or territories including New Mexico. Further complications were caused by Congress in its creation of the Colorado territory in 1861 that lopped off the northern most portion of New Mexico. Then in 1863, Congress severed off the western portion of the New Mexico territory to create the territory of Arizona.

In 1891, Congress finally admitted the failures of the Surveyors General in the territories and created the Court of Private Land Claims. Juan had commented sarcastically that forty three years after the Treaty of Guadalupe Hidalgo, the U.S. was still trying to protect Hispanic land rights. The creation of this court came too late for those many Hispanic land grant holders who had died waiting or those whose land grants were taken from them.

NATURAL RESOURCES—

WITHIN THE LAW OF THE COMMONS? —Unknown

CHAPTER 19
A NATIONAL PARK

ON THE PORTAL of the Buenavida home, Maria and Marcos were sitting and awaiting their turn at their father's vigil. They both were commiserating over their father's coma and how they couldn't believe this had happened to someone who had seemed so invincible to them.

"Do you remember how Papá always seemed to be aware of the latest news in the U.S. and world"? asked Marcos.

"Yes", replied Maria, "and we were able to ask Papá questions about any of the news during our after- dinner talks".

"And remember how we learned to read the newspapers Papá had ordered from the east", said Marcos. "Those newspapers were our windows to the world".

"And do you remember how we had that big discussion, over several nights about a U.S. national park being created"? Maria asked.

"Yes, I think it was in 1872", replied Marcos. "It was all about President Grant persuading Congress to create a new national park called Yellowstone in the state of Wyoming. Papá had to explain to us that the United States nor any other country had ever done something like that before. He tried to get us to understand how significant it was for a government to actually take a very large area of public land, about 3,500 square miles, out of probable development around fragile and scenic attractions. Yellowstone had unique geothermal features like geysers and much wildlife within its borders. What typically had previously happened in the U.S. was that such an attraction would have become privately owned and the public would have had to pay to see it. Plus in the rush to maximize the owner or developer's profits, roads and railroads would have been built to the attraction and hotels installed right next to it. Papá mentioned the sad example of Niagara Falls in New York State where this had actually occurred".

"And recall how we kids asked Papá what was wrong with enabling lots of people to see the attraction", interjected Maria. "He patiently explained that something beautiful needs to be protected and preserved for future generations to enjoy. He said that only the government could do that as a trustee for all the people, both those living now and future generations. Private owners or developers, he said, usually were blinded by the greed of maximizing profits quickly and if their over-development harmed or destroyed the attraction, too bad".

"Papá had also explained the early English practice of creating a "commons" (open public parkland) in many of their towns. These "commons" could not be built on and were to be enjoyed and owned by the public, but protected by the town government. These commons usually became inner city parks, like the large Central Park in New York City, as the towns grew. Papá told us that this English practice very probably was the ideological genesis for Congress creating Yellowstone".

"And remember that Papá went on to explain to us that Congress still was worried about private parties exploiting the newly created Yellowstone National Park", added Marcos. "He told us that Congress directed the U.S. Army to reside within the park in order to patrol and protect it against poachers and trespassers".

"And Yellowstone was just the first of many national parks to be later created by the Congress", said Maria. "I hope we get to visit some of them someday".

IF CATS WERE BORN IN AN OVEN, WOULD THEY BE BISCUITS? —U.S. v. Wong Kim Ark (1898), in which the U.S. Supreme Court held that all Chinese who were born in the U.S. were citizens.

CHAPTER 20
A COUNTRY FOR EVERYONE?

HIS FATHER'S COMA was in its fifth day and Tomás began to despair. His father had not been fed for fear of his choking- how long could one survive without food? Does being comatose require less sustenance? Tomás had no answer for his inner questions.

Tomás decided to walk out to the family cemetery after completing his turn at the vigil. Many of the visitors- relatives, friends, and neighbors- were smoking heavily on the portal. The cigarette smoke gave Tomás a headache. He was so thankful that his parents had strictly forbidden that nasty practice in his family. He personally could not understand the pleasure smokers claimed was derived from inhaling hot tobacco gases into one's body. Plus, they had the added burden of hand-rolling their cigarettes themselves plus paying for the tobacco, cigarette paper, and matches.

Reaching the cemetery with its two small, white crosses, Tomás sat down next to the cottonwood tree and used it as a backrest. From this hill, Tomás had a good view of the valley and could see the gleaming Pecos River to the east as it meandered south. The meadowlarks were singing in the nearby fields, oblivious to his father's coma. Looking up, the cottonwood tree was ablaze with its golden leaves of autumn as he sat in its shade. He could also see the extent of the Buenavida lands, his parent's rancho, his farm and his brother Marcos' farm. He suddenly realized the scope of his father's life's achievement. From a meager beginning in 1850, the Buenavidas had persevered despite hostile Anglo neighbors and an indifferent U.S. government.

Tomás remembered how as a student he had always questioned his father about the clear dichotomy between what he was being taught at school and the reality of the discrimination he and other Hispanics experienced. It was almost an inside joke within the Alianza- his father being nicknamed "the Brown Americano"- due to his father always protesting that Hispanics should not call Anglos "Americanos", because we Hispanics were Americanos as well. He said the practice reinforced a second- class mentality among Hispanics.

Tomás had hoped the Civil War would have ended all discrimination in the U.S., especially as against Negroes. After all, the South's slavery system had been dismantled and the horrible loss of life during the war certainly underscored the country's commitment to equality. Even after the passage of the 14th, 15th, and 16th Amendments to the U.S. Constitution, Tomás remembered his father's prophetic prediction that discrimination would not end in the United States. And his father had been correct. The newspapers had described the "Jim Crow" laws in the South- really an institutionalizing of the hatred of the Negro. These laws requiring separate facilities and schools for Negroes, poll taxes and literacy tests to prevent Negroes from voting, and so on, were enacted throughout the former Confederate states. Tomás remembered asking his father why the defeated southerners could not move on and forget their racist past. His father replied that the Confederates had, in fact, rationalized their hatred of the Negro—if someone can be bought and sold as property, how could they be equal to a White person? His father even predicted that these southerners would look back on the Civil War with pride and characterize it as their "heritage", to be celebrated, not forgotten as a treasonous and bigoted episode in our nation's history.

Tomás then had read about the Chinese Exclusion Act of 1882 that in effect prohibited all Chinese immigration at a time the United States was allowing immigration from all other countries. This law was a backlash to the large numbers of Chinese who had come to the United States during the 1850's for the California Gold Rush and then later to work on the building of railroads. The ability of the Chinese to work hard at low wages and survive harsh conditions – all caused resentment and hatred. The fact that the Chinese workers by custom boiled their water for tea probably immunized them from all the water-born diseases afflicting the Anglo workers.

The states were even more discriminatory, Tomás had learned. California enacted anti-Chinese laws which prohibited Chinese from holding jobs other than operating laundries, denied Chinese the right to bring criminal or civil charges against Whites and denied Chinese the right to own property. No wonder the Chinese huddled together in "China Towns" all along the west coast for safety and survival. The joke in California was that if someone had no chance at all, it was like having a "Chinaman's luck".

The federal law, Tomás learned, also denied U.S. citizenship to long- term Chinese residents. Many nationalized Chinese citizens had their U.S. citizenship revoked. "What drives such hatred of a targeted people", Tomás often wondered. He would have long discussions with his father seeking to understand how this behavior could exist in the U.S. with its lofty proclamations of equality and justice for all. His father had one explanation- "Hijo, I think it all goes back to the Pilgrims. They were expelled from England not because of their religious beliefs, but because they, the Pilgrims, discriminated against anyone who didn't believe as they did. When they arrived in the U.S., the Pilgrims continued to discriminate—first against the Indians, then the Negroes, the Irish, the Hispanics, and now the Chinese". Tomás could not argue against that logic.

MY MIND AND MY BODY AND MY SOUL, ALL TOTALLY

COMMITTED TO THE PROCESS. —Iain Pears, <u>The Portrait</u>,

describing an artist's epiphany in painting a picture well

CHAPTER 21
THE RAFFAELLO

MARIA WAS ENJOYING a cup of coffee in the quiet of her parent's living room – the kitchen had been, as usual, a circus of animated conversations amid the wonderful aromas of delicious food. She had just completed her turn at the vigil and wanted a little quiet.

As she sipped her coffee, she glimpsed the Raffaello (Raphael) oil painting gleaming on the wall opposite her as the afternoon sun's rays spotlighted it. Her father had purchased the painting, a good copy, in Mexico City when he left the university.

Her father called it the <u>Madonna of the Meadow</u>. He had discussed it several times when Maria and her brothers had been in school. He told them that Raffaello had been the best artist of the Renaissance, the art period between the Gothic of the 12th and 13th century and the Baroque of the 17th. He had been a contemporary of Michelangelo and Leonardo da Vinci, although both were much older than Raffaello.

Her father had lovingly described this painting Raffaello painted in 1506. His art class professor at the university, an Italian, had discussed Raffaello's paintings for a month. In this painting, the Madonna wore a red dress symbolizing Christ's death with a blue mantle- blue being the traditional color of heaven. He told them that we Catholics believe the Madonna, the Virgin Mary, is the top saint. So, the correlation of her in blue was that of the top saint in heaven. The painting had a triangular perspective, with the Madonna at the peak and the Christ child and his cousin, John the Baptist as a child, forming the two sides of the base. The Madonna is counterposed as she holds the Christ child as he reaches out to hold the small cross held by the child John. They are all surrounded by a shimmering green meadow with a beautiful and brilliant blue sky overhead.

Maria gazed at the small painting and smiled. She and her siblings had looked at each other as their father had gone on and on about this Raffaello painting. She had always liked it then, but now as a mother herself, she appreciated the spirituality it evoked. Perhaps it was that same sense of spirituality that had enthused her father so, some fifty years ago. Maria had recently visited the county library and learned that Raffaello had died at the very young age of thirty seven, but the quality of his work was so profound that he was still synonymous with the Renaissance— in French meaning the rebirth — of art in Europe. Maria suddenly thought- had she ever thanked her father for sharing his love of this art piece?

ENJOY THE LITTLE THINGS IN LIFE, FOR ONE

DAY YOU WILL LOOK BACK AND REALIZE

THEY WERE THE BIG THINGS. —Unknown

CHAPTER 22
THE FAMILY PICNIC

ANGELINA WAS DAYDREAMING. In the late afternoons of the vigil, she forced herself to recall pleasant memories rather than contemplate Juan's coma.

One of her fondest memories was of the family picnics on the banks of the Rio Negro. She and Juan would usually invite another family to join them- one of Juan's siblings or one of Angelina's. Several of the families had children close in age to their three children- the young cousins loved to play together, especially away from the usual home settings.

By wagon, the Rio Negro was about one hour south of the Buenavida rancho. The river's headwaters began in the Guadalupe Mountains to the west and its short course of thirty miles or so ended when it flowed into the Pecos. The family had one favorite picnic area at the Rio Negro- a wide bend in the river that formed a wide beach on the river's north bank shaded by many large cottonwood trees.

Angelina remembered a particular picnic in the late summer in 1865. She remembered it had been late summer because they had loaded watermelons and cantaloupes to have at the picnic. Her children had been ten to thirteen years old and Juan wanted to conclude the children's swimming lessons.

Juan had been adamant that their children learn to swim. He had read story after story in the eastern newspaper about hundreds of passengers drowning when ships capsized, often in sight of land. The large majority of people in the United States did not know how to swim.

The swimming lessons at the Rio Negro had begun when the children were toddlers. Juan and Angelina had encouraged the children to learn how to dog-paddle to each parent so that the fear of the water could be neutralized. Over the years, Juan and Angelina had taught the children to coordinate their arm and leg strokes and swim longer and longer distances. The children were also taught to float on the water- Juan repeatedly admonishing them that they could always float if they ever tired of swimming.

The Buenavida picnic beach had the added feature of a cottonwood tree branch that protruded out over the river. A rope had long ago been tied to that branch which allowed anyone to swing over and drop into the river. The rite of passage for the children had been to have the courage to not only swing and drop into the river, but be able to swim back to the shore.

Angelina recalled how proud she and Juan were when Marcos, their youngest, accomplished the feat. They had stood side by side on the bank as he had dropped into the river yelling loudly while everyone cheered him on. As he surfaced, he immediately started swimming confidently to the shore. Ten or so strokes later had him smiling and standing on the shore.

Angelina smiled to herself as she recalled her terror when Juan had first started the swimming lessons for the children. He had taught them to dog-paddle as he held them. Soon thereafter, Juan had told each of the children that he was going to throw them away from him, into the deep river and they had to prove to themselves they could dog- paddle back to him. Angelina had been in the river with Juan and she recalled the mother's panic she felt as each child was thrown and disappeared beneath the river's surface. But having been properly trained, each child quickly had surfaced already dog- paddling and confidently grinning as they swam back to their father.

Yes, those had been happy times for her and Juan. She realized that parents live vicariously through their children. She and Juan had been blessed with four beautiful children, the three survivors of whom now had rewarded them with beautiful, intelligent, and kind grandchildren.

OUR FAMILY IS A BLESSING, IT SHARES

SO MANY THINGS. —Unknown

CHAPTER 23
AN ENGLISH LESSON

IT HAD BEEN difficult learning English at home. Tomás Buenavida chuckled to himself as he rode his horse home from his parent's rancho. He and his siblings had just been reminiscing during their visit at their parents' home- who had learned the most, or who had mastered the English alphabet the quickest.

Their father had been exceedingly patient with them and their mother. He had explained that while Spanish words are pronounced based on the sounds of their constituent letters, and how the word "looks", many English words are not. And with many English words, the context in which the words are used in a sentence, determines their proper pronunciation and meaning.

Maria had reminded them how their father had illustrated the last point. He had waited until they all could recite the alphabet and could pronounce the sounds of each English letter. Then he had written the following sentence on each of their writing tablets: "Since there is no time like the present, he thought it was time to present the present." The word "present" was underlined in the sentence. Their father then had asked each of them, in turn, to read the sentence out loud. They had all pronounced the word "present" the same in all three places in the sentence.

Their father then read the same sentence and they all heard the different pronunciations of the word. He had explained that the first and third uses of the word in the sentence were as nouns and in the second use, it was as a verb. They had then realized the nuances of proper English pronunciation- one had to know the different meanings of the same spelled word and how it was used – it's context in a sentence- in order to pronounce it correctly.

They had asked their father for another example. He then had written the following sentence on their tablets: "When shot at, the dove dove into the bushes". Again they were each asked to read the sentence aloud. This time some of them understood the two meanings of the same spelled word and pronounced the word differently.

By the time the Buenavida children began attending the village public school, they had a good foundation in English and could read and write it. Their one teacher had even acknowledged to Angelina and Juan the excellent home schooling the children had received.

AGUA POR LOS BUEYES, VINO POR LOS REYES.

(Water for the oxen, wine for the kings) —an old Spanish saying

CHAPTER 24
NEW MEXICO HISPANIC "CHISTOS"

CHISTOS AND STORY-TELLING was almost an art form among the Hispanic families in southeastern New Mexico. Whenever the Buenavidas had company for dinner, it was customary for the guests and the hosts to sit around after dinner and tell stories or pose chistos (riddles). The Buenavida and other children would be invited to sit quietly on the perimeter of the adult discussions.

Marcos Buenavida's favorite story was "La Bruja" (the Witch) which he first heard told by his grandmother Vigil when he was an early teenager:

There was once a family in Malaga who had a beautiful daughter named Elena Gonzales. She had a boyfriend named David. This David had already asked her parents for Elena's hand in marriage. They had been dating for a considerable period of time.

Now there was another young girl in Malaga, named Philipa, who loved David very much, but David was in love with Elena.

A dance was held in Malaga which David and Elena attended. As Elena and David were dancing, Philipa arrived and approached them. Philipa said, "How pretty you look tonight Elena" and then reached out and quickly touched the necklace Elena was wearing. Elena thanked Philipa for the compliment and Philipa left the dance. The next day Elena became very ill, fell into a coma and began to lose weight. Her family sought medical treatment, but the doctors could not determine what was causing Elena's condition.

At this time, an elderly woman in Malaga, a Doña Andrea, was known to be both a "curandera" and a very religious person who had the power of prayer. In desperation, Elena's parents requested Doña Andrea's help.

Doña Andrea went to Elena's bedside and began to pray the rosary for her with her gathered family and friends. After a few days of Doña Andrea's intercession, Elena began to show signs of improvement.

On the fourth day, Doña Andrea was walking to Elena's home when Doña Maria, Philipa's mother approached her on the road. Doña Maria said, "Where are you going Andrea"? Doña Andrea replied that she was going to pray for Elena. Doña Maria then said, "Why do you go since it's a lost cause"? Before Doña Andrea could respond, Doña Maria quickly said, "You have something crawling on your neck" and quickly reached out with her hand and touched Doña Andrea's neck as if to brush something off. After Doña Andrea thanked her, they both went their separate ways.

Within a few minutes, as Doña Andrea arrived at Elena's house, her neck became inflamed and swollen, with the result being that Doña Andrea could not speak or pray out loud. The doctors Doña Andrea consulted could not treat her or determine why her neck was so inflammed and swollen. Doña Andrea's condition lasted one week during which time Elena died.

A few months after Elena's death, David married Philipa. Many of Malaga's residents knew that Philipa's mother practiced witchcraft and had orchestrated all these events.

Maria Buenavida liked the chistos and how some of the riddles were phonetically based while others were trickier. Some of her favorites were:

1. "Tu allá y yo aquí.

Que es?

Answer: La toalla"

(You there and me here. What is it? Answer: the towel)

2. "Entre más grande, menos se ve.

Que Es?

Answer: la noche"

(As it gets longer, the less you see of it. What is it? Answer: The night)

3."Largo, largo y crucificado, todos andan, y el parado.

Que es?

Answer: El camino"

(Long, long and criss-crossed, everyone walks and he stands still. What is it? Answer: the road)

4."En una cuevita, hay una tablita, todo el tiempo esta mojadita.

Que es?

Answer: La lengua"

(In a little cave, there is a little board which is always a little wet. What is it? Answer: the tongue)

5."Que hace el buey cuando el sol sale?

Answer: Su sombra "

(What does the ox make when the sun comes out? Answer: It's shadow)

6."Redondito, Redondón, no tiene tapa ni tapón.

Que es?

Answer: El anillo"

(A little round and very round, with no lid or stopper. What is it? Answer: the ring)

7. "Pelos con pelos y pelon adentro.

Que es?

Answer: El ojo"

(Hairs against hairs yet hairless inside. What is it? Answer: the eye)

8. "San Juanito va y San Juanito viene y Doña Margarita abierta, te lo tiene.

Que Es?

Answer: Un balde en una noria"

(St. John comes and St. John goes while Doña Margarita has it open for you. What is it? Answer: a bucket in a well)

9. "Fui a la tienda y merque d'ella, vine a la casa y lloré con ella.

Que es?

Answer: La cebolla"

(I went to the store and bought some of it, then I came home and cried with it. What is it? Answer: the onion)

10."Agua pasa por mi casa

Acate de mi corazón

Si no me lo adivinan

Como son cabezon.

Ques es?

Answer: el aguacate"

(Water passes by my home

Revered by my heart,

If you don't figure it out

You are all stupid fools.

What is it?

Answer: the avocado)

Maria and her brothers often had the chisto teller repeat the riddle as some of them, like the last one, could be solved by phonetically sounding out the key words- here "agua" and "acate"— to get to the answer: "aguacate".

NAMASTE—I HONOR THE SPIRIT IN YOU, WHICH IS ALSO IN ME. —Hindu saying

CHAPTER 25
INDIAN POLICY

ALIANZA MEETINGS WERE mostly social and educational events for the Hispanic family members. After 1850, these families in the southeastern corner of the new territory of New Mexico were isolated and they were aware of it. Unlike the Hispano communities along El Camino Real in the Rio Grande river valley, the Alianza families did not have the legacy of Hispanic settlements or government. The old saying of "Poor New Mexico, so far from Heaven and so close to Texas" seemed to have been coined just for this area of New Mexico adjacent to the Texas panhandle.

Due to the constant fear of Indian raids, the Alianza requested that Juan speak about U.S. Indian policy at one of its first meetings.

Juan began by reviewing Spanish Indian policy: "The Pueblo Indian revolt in 1680 resulted primarily because the Franciscan priests had advised the Spanish governors in Santa Fe to prohibit Pueblo Indian religious practices and dances. The Pueblo Indians, as a result, blamed the Spanish for all their troubles- droughts causing crop losses and raids by Navajos and Comanches- if they could have had their religious ceremonies and dances, these evil events would not have occurred.

"After the reconquest, the Spanish had learned their lesson- they needed the Pueblos as allies, not enemies. In the 1700's, the Pueblo Indians were allowed to maintain their language and ancient religious practices- the influence of the Catholic Church on Indian policy was greatly reduced. Spain also wanted its New Mexico colony to flourish- it needed it and California to serve as a buffer against the French, English, and Russian expansion efforts in North America.

"By the mid-1700's, Spanish New Mexico had only five thousand Hispanics. Why? Because all the Spanish settlements were under constant attack by the Comanche on the east, the Ute and Navajo to the west and northwest, and the Apache to the south. The biggest threat was the Comanche. The Spanish government directed Juan Bautista de Anza, the newly appointed New Mexico Governor in 1778, to defeat the Comanche and obtain a peace treaty protecting the New Mexico settlements. In 1779, Governor de Anza and his army of Spanish soldiers, aided by hundreds of Pueblo Indians, chased and killed the most powerful of the Comanche chiefs, "Cuerno Verde" (Green Horn) in the defeat of his tribe in a battle in what is now southeastern Colorado. It then took seven years to negotiate a formal peace treaty in 1786 with the Comanche since Spain's attention was diverted to helping the American colonies and their revolution against the hated English. Remember, it was the English that were constantly attacking Spanish ships returning to Spain heavily laden with silver and other treasure. Surprisingly, the Comanche honored the peace treaty with Spain and the Hispano communities expanded in New Mexico.

"Beginning in 1850, the United States policy toward the Indians was initially to eradicate them. A series of U.S. Army Forts- Fort Union (just north of Las Vegas), Fort Marcy in Santa Fe, Fort Sumner (south of Santa Rosa), Fort Craig (south of Socorro) and Fort Fillmore (near Mesilla) – were established to try to control and defeat the warring tribes. After the Civil War, the U.S. policy became one of forcibly resettling the warring and nomadic tribes onto fixed reservations.

"The biggest factor differentiating the Spanish and United States approaches- the United States threw more soldiers into the fight. And by establishing forts strategically, the U.S. Army could respond and move quickly after Indian raids.

"Compadres," Juan had concluded, "having Fort Stockton and its Army patrols to our south has protected us. That and Spanish Governor de Anza's defeat of the Comanche in the 1770's".

Juan had closed by stressing that the Alianza members might still be vulnerable to Indian raids and warned everyone to be vigilant and remember their alarm system.

THE REWARD OF A THING WELL DONE IS TO HAVE

DONE IT. —Emerson

CHAPTER 26
"DON PANCHITO"

ONE OF THE frequent visitors to the vigil was Don Luis Parras, a silver haired, stooped over gentleman in his early nineties. Don Luis was a long time widower who grazed sheep on the south side of the Rio Negro, just west of its confluence with the Pecos River. He would shuffle over to Angelina and pay his respects and inquire as to Juan's condition. He would then return to a corner chair of the bedroom.

In his left hand, Don Luis always brought with him his best friend, "Don Panchito". Don Panchito was a pet black crow which would gaze out from his perch in a small, straw colored wicker cage carried by Don Luis. Angelina had heard that this was in fact the third Don Panchito that Don Luis had had.

Don Panchito was in fact famous in the Malaga area. He and his two predecessors had been raised as young birds by Don Luis and taught to talk. Don Luis accomplished this feat by having learned an old Yaqui Indian technique of cutting off, at an angle, the baby crow's tongue. After the tongue healed, Don Luis would talk to the baby crow constantly repeating words or phrases. As a result of its shortened tongue, the crow's usual "Caw" call became sounds mimicking the human words Don Luis kept repeating. Similar to the training of parrots, the incessant word sounding by Don Luis resulted in Don Panchitos which could "talk" by responding to questions or word cues.

Don Panchito was also trained to fly to and stay on Don Luis' left shoulder upon a hand signal. Angelina had heard that the Don Panchitos had free roam of Don Luis' home, but always would stay on his shoulder when outside. The residents of Malaga were accustomed to seeing Don Panchito talking to Don Luis. People would approach the crow and ask "Quien eres?" (who are you?) or "Como te llamas?" (what are you called?). The crow would respond clearly "Don Panchito, Don Panchito"- always twice. The crow's repertoire included saying "Estoy bien" (I am fine), "Buenos Dias" (Good day), and "Hola" (Hello).

Besides being a talking crow, this latest Don Panchito was also famous for saving Don Luis' sheep. Reportedly, Don Luis, as always, had placed Don Panchito in his cage on a large rock near where he had spread his blanket to sleep. Nearby, the sheep were huddled together. Sometime in the night, several coyotes were circling and approaching the sleeping flock. The crow heard and/or saw the coyotes and called out his name loudly and repeatedly. Don Luis quickly awoke and scared away the predators. For weeks, Don Luis told everyone about his pet's heroism.

I USED TO SAY, WHEN I WAS YOUNG,

THAT TRUTH WAS THE MAJORITY VOTE OF THAT

NATION THAT COULD LICK ALL OTHERS.

—Oliver Wendell Holmes, National Law, 32 Harv. L.R. 40 (1918)

CHAPTER 27
SPANISH- AMERICAN WAR

ON THE FIFTH day of Juan's coma, Frank Johnson, Jr. a cattle rancher from Loving arrived to pay his respects. His father had helped the Buenavidas on their move to New Mexico in 1850 and had been a good friend of Juan's. In fact, Juan and Angelina had attended the senior Johnson's funeral in 1895.

After speaking to Angelina, Frank was greeted by Marcos who invited him into the kitchen for some coffee. Marcos liked Frank, Jr. who was just a few years older than he and had been a frequent visitor along with his father to the Buenavida rancho.

"Marcos, I sincerely hope your father recovers from his coma soon", Frank, Jr. said as he and Marcos sat down with their coffee.

"Thank you", Marcos replied. "With all those family members and friends in there praying, my Dad has a lot of us pulling for him," Marcos added. Changing the subject, Marcos said "Frank, how was your service as a Rough Rider in Cuba"?

"Ah, the Spanish-American War", Frank replied. "Yes, we haven't really talked about it, have we? Well, first, remember that war only lasted four months, April to August of 1898. The Treaty of Paris formally ended the war when it was signed in December, 1898".

"But, didn't you have a hard time getting your father's permission to volunteer"? interjected Marcos.

"Yes", Frank replied, "My father didn't believe in the war. He thought it was all a classic example of "yellow journalism"- the New York newspapers owned by Hearst and Pulitzer were competing against each other for readership by sensationalizing the facts and swaying public opinion to demand a war against Catholic Spain and its fight to put down "rebels seeking independence for Cuba".

"But I thought the U.S. and Spain had agreed on a solution for Cuba", Marcos asked. "I remember reading that President McKinley and the business community didn't want a war with Spain- they just wanted peace in Cuba since the rebels were hurting the U.S. owned sugar and rum businesses there. In fact, hadn't Spain and the U.S. agreed to Cuban autonomy effective in January, 1898"?

"Yes, that's correct and it was being implemented until the U.S.S. Maine exploded in Havana Harbor in February", Frank answered. "Two hundred sixty six sailors were killed and the U.S. newspapers fueled the fire with headlines of "Remember the Maine- to hell with Spain!" President McKinley was in effect forced by Congress and public opinion to sign joint resolutions of Congress authorizing U.S. forces to evict Spain if it didn't voluntarily withdraw".

"That's right", Marcos added. "And Spain had no choice but to declare war against the U.S. since Cuba was its sovereign territory. And of course, the U.S. responded by declaring war against Spain the next day. Too bad that the U.S. didn't remember all the critical support it received from Spain during the Revolutionary War. You know it was General Bernardo Gálvez who as Governor of Louisiana first sealed off the port of New Orleans to British ships in 1777 so they could not re-supply their forts along the Mississippi River. Then after Spain declared war against Great Britain in 1779, it was Gálvez that captured those British forts at Baton Rouge and Natchez. He accomplished this by utilizing an unique army comprised of Spanish soldiers, free Blacks, Creoles and American Indians. In 1780, Gálvez attacked and captured the British fort at Mobile, Alabama and the year later the British Gulf capitol at Pensacola, Florida. Gálvez also sent much needed supplies and money to General Washington. And that's not all. General Gálvez then helped draft the treaty that ended the American revolution and gave the United States its freedom.—how quickly we forget history".

"Yes Marcos, it makes you wonder but it also is surprising that most U. S. history books don't even mention Gálvez. But back to Cuba. Did you know that the U.S. at that time had less than thirty thousand men in the Army"? asked Frank. "The government had to activate the state national guards and recruit volunteers like me to form the Rough Riders".

"So, how did the U.S. troops do in Cuba against Spain's forces"? asked Marcos. "Isn't Cuba a hot and humid tropical island"?

"Well, it was a real disaster on the ground", replied Frank, shaking his head. "First, the regular Army types tried to use the old Civil War frontal battle lines and suffered many losses since the Spanish fought a guerilla style of warfare. The Spanish had learned this method after several years of fighting the Cuban rebels. The Rough Riders under Colonel Teddy Roosevelt had more success since we were Calvary and could adjust quickly. "Second, within weeks, up to half of all U.S.

forces in Cuba came down with malaria and jungle fever- they couldn't fight anyone".

"So, how did the U.S. win this war in four months"? asked Marcos.

"We have the U.S. Navy to thank for that" ,replied Frank. "They quickly destroyed the Spanish fleet and without supplies the Spanish land forces had no choice but to surrender".

"And to the victor goes the prize", interjected Marcos. "I remember Spain was forced to cede Puerto Rico, the Philippine Islands, and Guam to the U.S., plus give up its sovereignty over Cuba. The U.S. did pay Spain $20 million- a sop to Spanish pride".

"So, Frank, did anyone figure out what caused the sinking of the U.S.S. Maine"? asked Marcos.

"You know several inquires were conducted regarding the sinking of the U.S.S. Maine", replied Frank. "One found the cause to be an internal explosion; the other concluded the ship hit a mine. Either way, the U.S. had no legal right to send one of its warships into a Spanish port. Regardless, as a result of its victory, the U.S. became an international power with its empire spreading into the Pacific. Spain's world standing and power were greatly diminished as a result. No wonder us "Gringos" aren't so popular in most Spanish-speaking countries", Frank joked.

"I remember my father teaching us Buenavida kids what "gringo" meant", Marcos said. "It really just means an Anglo, a non-Hispanic, but in light of the Mexican War and the Spanish-American War, it is much more of a negative term when applied to U.S. anglo citizens. This sentiment also explains why so few U.S. Hispanics volunteered to fight against Spain".

"Well Marcos, I need to head home", Frank said as he stood up. "Thanks for the coffee and conversation. I hope and pray your father recovers, and soon".

Marcos escorted his friend outside. "I'll convey your well wishes to my mother, Frank. Come visit again".

IT'S CHOICE, NOT CHANCE

THAT DETERMINES YOUR DESTINY. —Jean Nidetch

CHAPTER 28
THE CATTLE BUSINESS

THE BUENAVIDAS USUALLY operated a herd of 200 cattle and at least three breeding bulls. That number plus the annual calf production allowed the family to drive and sell seventy-five to one hundred head of cattle to the area U.S. forts on an annual basis. The Army usually paid above the going rate for the Mexican range cattle since their forts were not near cattle ranches. In the mid-1850's the cattle were sold by the Buenavidas for $6 a head rising to $8 a head in the mid-1860's and $11 a head by the mid-1870's. The Army always paid in U. S. silver dollars. This income supported the Buenavidas for the year.

Soon after Juan and Angelina's marriage, the Buenavida rancho had to begin branding its cattle. The family's branding iron, a capital "B" inside a "V" had been forged in Mexico by Juan's father and met a brand's two main objectives—a clearly recognized symbol and one not easily subject to alteration. A cattleman's fear was theft by way of re-branding his cattle to the thief's brand.

Branding had been made necessary due to the open- range grazing the Buenavidas utilized. Also, neighboring Alianza families and Anglo ranchers also open-grazed cattle of their own. A long fence had been placed to the south of the Buenavida house to protect gardens from the cattle. The fence consisted of long pine tree trunks (vigas) placed abeam stone piles four feet in height. The fence had required several wagon expeditions to the nearby Guadalupe Mountains to harvest the trees. The completed fence stretched east to west across the Buenavida rancho.

Besides the annual branding, the other major challenge for the family was calving. The Buenavidas had to be vigilant since a breach birth might present itself and risk both the calf and cow's lives. Here, the Buenavida women were invaluable. First, Lucia had taught Angelina and then Angelina had taught Maria how to respond quickly. Their small hands enabled them to reach into the birthing cow's uterus and turn the breached calf into the proper position. All the Buenavida men knew to quickly alert the women if they saw a birthing cow with a possible breach.

Like most of their neighbors, the Buenavidas used a smokehouse to dry and cure beef. The Buenavida women would cut the fresh meat into thin strips that would be placed on vertical wood racks in the adobe smoke-house. Dried mesquite bush roots would be burned to produce the high heat and smoke for the meat. Usually, two days of smoking was required to properly cure the meat and make the beef jerky. Besides the infrequent fresh beef, the Buenavida kitchen utilized the dried beef in stews, chiles and beans. Angelina preferred fresh chicken despite having to behead the fowl and pluck the animal. The Buenavidas always had chickens and pigs for the kitchen as they were bartered to them for fresh or dried beef.

The daily routine for the Buenavida men was to watch over the cattle, round up strays, drive them to grass, and once a day, drive them to the river for watering. Guarding against rattlesnakes and their bites, coyote attacks on calves, and thunder induced stampedes added additional stress on the men. In the summer, the herd was driven to the valleys of the Guadalupe Mountains to the west for the fresh grass that grew there at the higher elevations.

At one of his post dinner talks, Juan had told the family about his discussions with Frank Johnson, a Loving cattle rancher in 1871. "Señor Johnson tells me that the longest cattle drives he has heard of are the ones by the King Ranch of south Texas. That ranch is supposedly the largest ranch in the U.S. Every year it drives thousands of cattle for one hundred days from south Texas to Abilene, Kansas, the railroad railhead. At Abilene, an $11 a head Texas steer can be sold for $20 a head and it will be resold at Chicago's stock yards for $30 a head".

Tomás had asked how the men on the cattledrive were paid. Juan explained, "Señor Johnson says that the men are paid after the cattle are sold in Abilene. The King Ranch has the trail boss be responsible for the men's wages and the proceeds. The trail boss, in turn, is paid part of the profit realized by the King Ranch".

Juan concluded by telling the family that they may have to join in similar cattledrives with area ranchers if the U.S. forts near them were ever closed or stopped buying their cattle.

REMEMBER THE THREE "R's": RESPECT FOR SELF, RESPECT FOR OTHERS, AND RESPONSIBILITY FOR ALL YOUR ACTIONS. —Unknown

CHAPTER 29
A LIFE CODE

TOMÁS LOOKED AT his father from his vantage point along his parent's bedroom wall. He was awaiting his turn at the bedside vigil. His father looked at peace as he persisted in his coma, his slight breathing inaudible amongst all the quiet huddled discussions in the bedroom and the sound of cooking emanating from the always busy Buenavida kitchen.

Tomás suddenly focused on the realization that his father had been right all along. All of the family post-dinner talks his father had led dealing with a personal code to live by had been exemplified by his life. For example, his convincing his family to relocate to New Mexico from a hostile and bigoted Texas after the U.S.- Mexican War – it could not have been easy for them to leave the old family rancho and travel two hundred miles north with their possessions and cattle. But doing so protected and perpetuated the Buenavida family. The family was the most important element of his father's code. He would repeatedly tell them as children that if life were stripped of all its material possessions, what really mattered was one's family. Your spouse as a life partner, your children, and what you do to point them to a happy life, your parents and the moral obligation to care for them in their old age- that, he said, was what family was all about and what should concern and consume everyone of us.

With family as the life road we travel, Tomás recalled that being true to oneself was his father's second key life code element. Tomás remembered that he and his siblings had struggled with this abstract concept- what did their father mean? His father had explained over several sessions that being true to oneself had two different components which supported one another. The first component was to respect oneself. By this, his father had explained, he meant that each of us must try to live our life without compromising our principles- treating everyone fairly and with respect, not shirking our responsibilities, keeping our word, and being responsible for all our actions. If we remained true to these principles, we would not be ashamed of our actions, we would have no regrets, and consequently, we would respect ourselves and be true to ourselves.

But that component was not enough by itself. His father had then read the bible story of the Good Samaritan to them. He explained that both the priest and the rich Levite had walked on past the bleeding robbery victim on the road. But, it was the Samaritan who was moved by compassion to stop and care for the victim- tending to his wounds and then paying an innkeeper to care for the man. His father had explained that in Jesus' time, Samaritans were considered social and religious outcasts. Yet, it was a Samaritan that came to the aid of a Jew while the Levite, who was Jewish and rich enough to help, and the priest, who morally knew to help, had not done anything. His father went on to explain that in our time, it would be like a Negro coming to the aid of a white man.

His father then had told them that the second component of being true to oneself, was to love your neighbor as had the Good Samaritan. Inherent in this he went on, is to not hate anyone. He explained how he had been tempted to hate only once- when those Texan bounty hunters had arrived looking for Amos, the runaway slave. At that time, he had felt anger and hatred for these brutal men seeking to re-imprison a fellow human-being. He then explained that as those Texans rode back east across the Pecos river empty handed, he had caught himself and rethought his feelings. Even though his whole being recoiled against slavery, those men believed in the system and saw it as being crucial to their agricultural economy.

His father had finalized his point by telling them that, God willing, we all had sixty or seventy years to live on earth. This is such a short life time to spend one day of it hating anyone. His father had also explained that sometimes, in order to not hate, it is necessary to forgive. If we all forgave everything anyone had done to us, is there a reason to still hate? His father had concluded by saying, " Why not spend your energy and life helping others when you can"?

"If you decide to live your life such that you respect yourself, and you forgive all and not hate, then and only then", his father had said, "will you really be true to yourself".

Tomás reflected on his father's teachings and looking across the room, concluded that his father had practiced in his own life what he had preached. All the friends and neighbors attending his father's vigil were a testament to the good his father had done in his life. He had been true to himself.

EARTH CRIES, HEAVEN SMILES. —Santana, "Europa"

CHAPTER 30
THE MEXICAN REVOLUTION

MARCOS QUIETLY LEFT his parent's bedroom after finishing his turn at the vigil. He walked out on the portal and joined a small group of neighbors. They were discussing the 1910 Mexican revolution led by Francisco Madero against the dictator General Porfirio Díaz. Some of these neighbors were saying that the fighting in Mexico was so wide-spread they feared traveling to Chihuahua, much less further south. They were also discussing the large number of Mexicans coming across the border to avoid the revolution's bloodshed.

One of the neighbors, Alfonso Sanchez, turned to Marcos and asked if he knew how the revolution had started. Marcos, nodded his head, and replied: "Don Alfonso, we have to start a little earlier in history. My papá has discussed this with my family based on his studies at the university in Mexico City and recent newspaper stories. I should begin with the fact that Mexican politics have always been based on two opposing political philosophies—the liberals and the conservatives. The conservatives usually are comprised of the wealthy hacienda owners and business owners who usually are direct descendants of Europeans.

These people wanted to continue a monarchy in Mexico, headed up by an European monarch, after Mexico won its independence from Spain in 1821. The liberals, however, prevailed and elected Benito Juárez, a mixed blood Mexican as Mexico's first president. The liberals advocated for agrarian land reform, that is, breaking up the large haciendas owned by a few wealthy families and alloting land to the peasants, who were landless. They also demanded a democratically elected president and congress. Juarez served as president until his death in 1872 but had to survive a conservative led attempt to impose a French emperor on Mexico.

"General Díaz served as president from 1876 and was "re-elected" repeatedly until 1910. However, Díaz used his army to force people to vote for him or he simply rigged the election results. He knew he was violating the Mexican constitution by these methods but, as dictator, he did not want to relinquish power. In 1910, Madero, a son of a wealthy landowner but with liberal ideals, challenged Díaz for the presidency but was imprisoned by Díaz. Díaz then declared himself re-elected. Madero escaped from jail and issued a call for a revolution to expel Díaz, end continuous re-election, enact land reform and ensure free suffrage. His call was supported by many Indians, liberals and regional armies led by Pancho Villa, Emiliano Zapata, and Pascual Orozco. The combined armies of Madero and his allies defeated the federal army in May, 1911 and forced Díaz to abdicate and leave Mexico. Madero insisted on immediate elections which he won overwhelmingly. Madero established a democracy and is still the Mexican president. The United States quickly recognized his government".

The neighbors thanked Marcos for his explanation. Alfonso Sanchez expressed the hope that Mexico would now enter into a period of peace and prosperity for its people. Marcos agreed but stated "My papá says that Mexico has suffered a long history of exploitation of its people by the Spanish, the French, its own generals and dictators. The country needs to learn how to function as a democracy for several decades, with peaceful changes of democratically elected governments, so that its unfortunate history can be successfully overcome. We'll see if it can".

One of the other neighbors asked Marcos what will happen to the newly arrived Mexicans. Marcos replied " Well, they will not be eligible for automatic citizenship under the terms of the Guadalupe Hildalgo treaty since they came from Mexico and they will not be eligible for the 160 acre homestead grants since they were not here as of 1853. They will have to become naturalized citizens of the U.S. if they decide not to return to Mexico. My papá tells us that the U.S. Mexico border will be a very porous border for many years to come because of the economic hardships suffered by the Mexican people. The Mexican dictators have not allowed the vast population to own their own land and much of the country's wealth is owned by a small number of families. Until Mexico develops industry and work for its people, we can expect its citizens to come across the border into the United States in order to survive. And we must help them if we can. I believe they would help us if the tables were turned and we were forced to go work and live in Mexico in order to feed our families here". The neighbors all agreed with Marcos on that last point.

LOVE THE PEOPLE WHO TREAT YOU RIGHT;

FORGET ABOUT THE ONES WHO DON'T. —Unknown

CHAPTER 31
THE NAVARRETTE MATTER

AFTERNOONS WERE THE worst part of the day for Angelina. She would have served her turn at the vigil by Juan's bedside in the morning. After lunch, Angelina had four to five long hours of quiet discussions with friends and family or quiet contemplation.

This afternoon, the sixth day of Juan's coma, Angelina retreated to the portal which was deserted for once. Sitting on the wood bench there, she gazed out at the rancho and the sunny vistas to the south. She suddenly thought of the Navarrette family incident. The Alianza had evolved since its inception by developing a uniform barter value system for use by its members and by mediating member family disputes. The Navarrette incident had been one of the first Alianza mediations.

Antonio Navarrete's wife had died shortly after the birth of their sixth child, a daughter. This child was considerably younger than her siblings and Antonio, an Alianza member, was unable to care for her properly. Since he was planning to move his family to Chihuahua, Mexico, he went to his sister-in-law, Eloisa Duarte, and requested she take care of his newborn daughter. He promised to send money annually to reimburse the costs of her upbringing, food, and clothing. Antonio also promised he would personally return to take his daughter home when she was older or when he and his family would return to New Mexico. Antonio had leased his small farm to a neighbor, also an Alianza member.

Despite having a large family of her own, Antonio's sister-in-law agreed to care for her niece. The problem developed when, after a year from Antonio's departure, no money was received by Eloisa. After the second year of no assistance, Eloisa asked the Alianza for assistance.

Angelina remembered she and Juan had talked about the matter extensively. The only remedy available to the Alianza was the money from the lease of Antonio's farm. The Alianza discovered that the lessee was periodically travelling to Chihuahua and paying Antonio there. The question for the Alianza was whether to involve itself and correct the present injustice of Antonio neglecting his obligations to his daughter and to his sister-in-law.

Angelina and two other Alianza women had visited the little girl, Celestina, at the Duarte's home. The Duartes, while quite poor, clearly loved the little girl who called Eloisa her "Mamá". Celestina appeared to be a happy member of the Duarte family. Her clothes were clearly "hand-me-down" and showed much wear.

Some members of the Alianza voiced concern about the Alianza's authority to interfere with a private lease contract. Others pointed out that Antonio Navarrette was clearly shirking his parental duties and since he was in Mexico, the only recourse was the lease money. Others pointed to the hardship the Duartes were experiencing with an additional child to feed and care for.

Angelina had explained to Juan that the real concern in the matter was the long-term emotional damage the little girl might suffer if she learned her father and her siblings had abandoned her. Angelina had asked Eloisa if she planned to tell Celestina about her real family when she was old enough to understand. Eloisa had responded that she didn't know what to do. If Antonio ever did return and Celestina had not been told, she, Eloisa, would be blamed. On the other hand, if she did tell Celestina and Antonio never came for her, the little girl would be scarred forever. Celestina would grow up always wondering why her father and family had abandoned her.

After several meetings and much debate, the Alianza voted to seize a small portion of Antonio Navarrette's annual lease payment to pay for his daughter's upbringing. Each Alianza family had one vote and a simple majority had decided the matter. To satisfy some Alianza members' concern, the seized money would be distributed quarterly to the Duartes by a committee of Alianza women who would ensure the funds were benefitting Celestina. The Alianza also agreed to defend the lessee against any claim by Antonio for incomplete lease payments. The Alianza's seizures of the monies were to continue until Antonio returned for his daughter, the lease was terminated, or Celestina died or married.

Angelina smiled to herself. That Navarrette incident and the Alianza's response had been difficult, but had made the group stronger. Juan had often commented that he was proud of how the Alianza had voted to do the right thing for that little girl. Angelina remembered that Celestina was never told of her real family, her father never came for her, and she ended up getting married at the age of sixteen as a Duarte.

LIFE IS NOT MEASURED BY THE NUMBER OF BREATHES WE TAKE, BUT BY THE MOMENTS THAT TAKE OUR BREATH AWAY. —Unknown

CHAPTER 32
SUNDAY PASEOS

EVEN WHEN THEIR children were still very young, Juan had initiated a custom that Angelina had, at first, not fully appreciated. Juan had insisted that they needed time alone, away from their home and the children, at least for a few hours each week.

At first, they had just ridden their horses to one of their favorite spots along one of the rivers and enjoyed each other's company on a blanket in the shade of one of the large cottonwood trees. Sunday afternoons were chosen as nothing was scheduled those days besides morning mass.

Angelina had felt uncomfortable leaving the children and had expressed her reservations to Juan. He said he understood her feelings but had explained that they both needed a break from the week's routine—she from the house work and being the caregiver; he from the rancho and all the work it represented. Just being away for a few hours, he said, would allow them to re-engage and focus on each other. Angelina understood what Juan was saying yet still felt a bit guilty leaving the children with Lucia.

But after a few months of their Sunday "paseos" (little journeys), Angelina was converted. She looked forward to the three to four hour escapes and the opportunity to converse with Juan without the distractions and interruptions the normal rancho life presented. She and Juan talked about the past week's events and the next week's challenges. They spoke about their children and their plans for their education. But the best times were when they just talked to each other as soul-mates, confiding in each other their hopes, fears and feelings. Looking at Juan as he spoke, Angelina more fully appreciated that they were, in fact, life partners. She and Juan were not only responsible for each other but for the lives and futures of their small children. The sense of responsibility they felt was overwhelming but somehow their love for each other seemed to give them the strength to persevere.

In 1876, Juan was able to trade some cattle for a small buggy of a neighbor. Big enough for the two of them and pulled by one horse, that buggy became the transport of choice for their Sunday paseos. Shortly after obtaining the buggy, Juan surprised the family after dinner by deciding to talk about Spanish carriage rides in Madrid in the 1600's. Juan had joked that their little buggy was only a poor cousin to the large fancy four and six horse carriages used in Madrid and other large Spanish cities. He related that he had read at the university about the social etiquette the "Madrileños" had developed for their carriage rides in the city. It was the custom on Saturday afternoons for the nobility and the wealthy to parade in their fine carriages along the broad "avenidas" (boulevards) of the capitol city. Depending on the occupant's marital status, age ,or social rank, the side curtains of the four to six person carriages would be fully or partially opened or closed. Everyone could easily ascertain the identities of the occupants—the carriages of the nobility were obvious by the uniformed footmen and drivers on the carriage and the wealthy displayed their family coat of arms on the carriage sides.

Juan had furthered explained that when the carriages slowly passed each other on the street, discreet signals or written notes could be quickly exchanged by the occupants. Juan had explained that the carriage parades in Madrid allowed its citizens to circumvent the strict societal rules which applied to unmarried women and members of the nobility. This was very similar to the Venetians and their use of masks during their pre-Lenten "Carnivale". During their two month party, the Venetians would dress themselves with fantastic masks to hide their true identity—this allowed Venetians of different economic or social order to mix freely and do all sorts of outrageous things.

As for the "Madrileños" and their carriage parades, Juan had commented that they were merely converting a mode of transportation into a social tool.

QUE DIOS BENDIGA CADA RINCÓN DE ESTA CASA.

(May God Bless Each Corner of This House)

—Old Spanish blessing

CHAPTER 33
A SURPRISE

IT WAS THE afternoon of the seventh day of Juan's coma. The bedroom was less crowded now- mostly family members. Juan's sisters still recited the rosary as they sat huddled in one corner. Angelina had had the village Catholic priest perform Last Rites for Juan the day before.

Angelina did not believe in a vengeful God. If Juan did not recover, it was because God was calling him home now. It was the same stoic pragmatism Angelina had earlier expressed after the loss of her second child. "Mi Dios se lo llevo" (My God took him), she would tell everyone.

In the late morning, Angelina was sitting near the bed, again holding Juan's hand and occasionally wiping his brow. The bandage on his head had been removed— her salve had worked its wonders on the gash. As she gazed at her husband, Angelina smiled. They had had a good life together. Four wonderful children, three of whom had survived and blessed them with grandchildren. Some of the younger grandchildren had attended the state's new land grant university in Las Cruces. Financially, they were well off— they owned their rancho and their cattle and had no debts.

Angelina leaned over and kissed Juan's cheek whispering "We did well, my husband". She again squeezed his hand as she had done throughout the vigil. Suddenly, Juan squeezed Angelina's hand. Angelina jumped up and fell out of her chair, crying out loudly "Juan just squeezed my hand! He's coming out of his coma"!

Everyone in the bedroom surrounded the bed and Tomás helped his mother to her feet. Tomás then quickly checked his father's wrist for a pulse and found none. He rechecked it at his father's neck- no pulse. Tomás then laid his ear on his father's chest- no heartbeat. He then embraced his mother saying, "He's gone, Mamá".

SURRENDER: EMBRACE WHATEVER COMES YOUR WAY.

—Unknown

CHAPTER 34
ASCENDING

JUAN COULD ALMOST hear himself thinking in the pitch darkness. Was he dead? All he could remember was his horse suddenly rearing up and jumping sideways so quickly that he had been thrown off— a rattlesnake striking? But if dead, why did he have this distinct sense of movement- very similar to the sensation of flying in the air after letting go of the rope swing over the Rio Negro. But then he was the one who decided when, in the swing's arc, to let go and fall into the river. Here he felt powerless, not in control. He felt as if he had been set in motion.

Suddenly, another flash of light enveloped him. As he adjusted to the flash of light, he saw Angelina in a bed holding a newborn baby— Tomás? She was looking up at him smiling with sweat glistening off her beautiful face. He only saw this vision briefly before darkness returned. He thought he had "seen" the vision, but did he have his eyes? Also, the visions, all of them, seemed real, as if he had gone back in time, to those events. He sensed he was and belonged there, at those places and times, in these flashbacks.

Without a frame of reference in the absolute blackness, Juan seemed to be slowing floating. Similar to the sensation of his body being carried by the Pecos River's strong current when he swam in it- but with no sound. Suddenly, another flash of light illuminated a graveside gathering of his family in 1891— his mother's funeral? Everyone in black, heads bowed, people crying. That scene had been right after all the eulogies. Just as suddenly, Juan was back in total darkness. He wondered if this was God's way of reminding him of his life- but why these specific scenes?

Another sudden flash of light showed him lying in his bed, eyes closed, with Angelina holding his hand. Their bedroom was filled with his children, family, friends, and neighbors. His Angelina! Just seeing her again took his breath away—just like the very first time he had met her. It had been when the Vigils had arrived to greet their new neighbors, the Buenavidas and to help them build their new home. Angelina still looked beautiful to him—the black dress she was now wearing made her look radiant. Angelina was leaning over and whispering to him. He could not hear what she was saying to him. If he could only say something to her or do something to let her know he loved her…….

Suddenly, Juan was again in total darkness and again moving. Above him, he sensed a break in the total darkness-almost like the earliest glimpse of a new dawn. He was also reminded of his cave exploring experiences as a young man in the Guadalupe Mountains- the relief he experienced in seeing a hint of the light coming from the cave's opening, after having felt lost in the cave's many twists and turns in the total darkness after his torch had gone out. But this soft light from above was different from the previous quick flashes preceding his visions- it was continuous now and getting progressively brighter. Juan, like a moth drawn to a light, felt as if he was now accelerating toward it. Juan's last thought as he was enveloped by a dazzling white light: "Ay, mi Dios"! (Oh, my God!)

Author's photograph by Carmen Schettino, Sarasota, Florida.

As a native New Mexican and a Hispanic, I personally experienced the assimilation challenges facing Hispanics in the southwest today. From that personal perspective, this book was written to explore the challenges Hispanic families experienced in the territory of New Mexico from 1850 to 1913. The motivation for the book was to preserve this history for Hispanic youth.

The author, Jose N. Uranga, is a retired environmental attorney living in Sarasota, Florida with his wife Joan. He has three children.